F

THE TWISTED THING

G·K
Hall
&Cº

Also published in Large Print
from G.K. Hall by Mickey Spillane:

Kiss Me, Deadly
The Killing Man

This Large Print Book carries the
Seal of Approval of N.A.V.H.

Mickey Spillane

THE TWISTED THING

G.K. Hall & Co.
Thorndike, Maine

Published in 1994 by arrangement with Dutton Signet,
a division of Penguin Books USA Inc.

G.K. Hall Large Print Mystery Collection.

The text of this Large Print edition is unabridged.
Other aspects of the book may vary from the original edition.

Set in 16 pt. News Plantin by Barbara Ingerson.

Printed in the United States on acid-free, high opacity paper.⊚

Library of Congress Cataloging in Publication Data

Spillane, Mickey, 1918–
    The twisted thing / Mickey Spillane.
      p.   cm.
    ISBN 0-8161-5556-9 (alk. paper : lg. print)
    ISBN 0-8161-5557-7 (alk. paper : lg. print : pbk.)
    1. Hammer, Mike (Fictitious character) — Fiction.
2. Private investigators — United States — Fiction. 3. Large
type books. I. Title.
[PS3537.P652T95   1994]
813'.54—dc20   93-38622

To Sid Graedon
who saw the charred edges

Chapter One

The little guy's face was a bloody mess. Between the puffballs of blue-black flesh that used to be eyelids, the dull gleam of shock-deadened pupils watched Dilwick uncomprehendingly. His lips were swollen things of lacerated skin, with slow trickles of blood making crooked paths from the corners of his mouth through the stubble of a beard to his chin, dripping onto a stained shirt.

Dilwick stood just outside the glare of the lamp, dangling like the Sword of Damocles over the guy's head. He was sweating too. His shirt clung to the meaty expanse of his back, the collar wilted into wrinkles around his huge neck. He pushed his beefy hand further into the leather glove and swung. The solid smack of his open hand on the little guy's jaw was nasty. His chair went over backward and his head cracked against the concrete floor of the room like a ripe melon. Dilwick put his hands on his hips and glared down at the caricature that once was human.

"Take him out and clean 'im up. Then get 'im back here." Two other cops came out of the darkness and righted the chair. One yanked the guy to his feet and dragged him to the door.

Lord, how I hated their guts. Grown men, they were supposed to be. Four of them in there taking turns pounding a confession from a guy who had nothing to say. And I had to watch it.

It was supposed to be a warning to me. Be careful, it said, when you try to withhold information from Dilwick you're looking for a broken skull. Take a look at this guy for example, then spill what you know and stick around so I, the Great Dilwick, can get at you when I want you.

I worked up a husky mouthful of saliva and spat it as close to his feet as I could. The fat cop spun on his heel and let his lips fold back over his teeth in a sneer. "You gettin' snotty, Hammer?"

I stayed slouched in my seat. "Any way you call it, Dilwick," I said insolently. "Just sitting here thinking."

Big stuff gave me a dirty grimace. "Thinking . . . you?"

"Yeah. Thinking what you'd look like the next day if you tried that stuff on me."

The two cops dragging the little guy out stopped dead still. The other one washing the bloodstains from the seat quit swishing the brush over the wicker and held his breath. Nobody ever spoke that way to Dilwick. Nobody from the biggest politician in the state to the hardest apple that ever stepped out of a pen. Nobody ever did because Dilwick would cut them up into fine pieces with his bare hands and enjoy it. That was Dilwick, the dirtiest, roughest cop who ever walked a beat or swung a nightstick over a skull. Crude, he was.

Crude, hard and dirty and afraid of nothing. He'd sooner draw blood from a face than eat and everybody knew it. That's why nobody ever spoke to him that way. That is, nobody except me.

Because I'm the same way myself.

Dilwick let out his breath with a rush. The next second he was reaching down for me, but I never gave him the chance to hook his hairy paws in my shirt. I stood up in front of him and sneered in his face. Dilwick was too damn big to be used to meeting guys eye to eye. He liked to look down at them. Not this time.

"What do you think you'll do?" he snarled.

"Try me and see," I said.

I saw his shoulder go back and didn't wait. My knee came up and landed in his groin with a sickening smash. When he doubled over my fist caught him in the mouth and I felt his teeth pop. His face was starting to turn blue by the time he hit the floor. One cop dropped the little guy and went for his gun.

"Cut it, stupid," I said, "before I blow your goddamn head off. I still got my rod." He let his hand fall back to his side. I turned and walked out of the room. None of them tried to stop me.

Upstairs I passed the desk sergeant still bent over his paper. He looked up in time to see me and let his hand snake under the desk. Right then I had my own hand six inches from my armpit practically inviting him to call me. Maybe he had a family at home. He brought his hand up on top of the desk where I could see it. I've seen eyes like his peering out of a rathole when there was a cat in the room. He still had enough I AM THE LAW in him to bluster it out.

"Did Dilwick release you?" he demanded.

I snatched the paper from his hand and threw it to the floor, trying to hold my temper. "Dilwick didn't release me," I told him. "He's downstairs vomiting his guts out the same way you'll be doing if you pull a deal like that again. Dilwick doesn't want *me*. He just wanted me to sit in on a cellar séance in legal torture to show me how tough he is. I wasn't impressed. But get this, I came to Sidon to legally represent a client who used his one phone call on arrest to contact me, not to be intimidated by a fat louse that was kicked off the New York force and bought his way into the cops in this hick town just to use his position for a rake-off."

The sergeant started to interrupt, licking his loose lips nervously, but I cut him short. "Furthermore, I'm going to give you just one hour to get Billy Parks out of here and back to his house. If you don't," and I said it slowly, "I'm going to call the State's Attorney and drop this affair in his lap. After that I'll come back here and mash your damn face to a pulp. Understand now? No habeas corpus, no nothing. Just get him out of here."

For a cop he stunk. His lower lip was trembling with fear. I pushed my hat on the back of my head and stamped out of the station house. My heap was parked across the street and I got in

10

and turned it over. Damn, I was mad.

Billy Parks, just a nice little ex-con trying to go straight, but do you think the law would help him out? Hell no. Let one thing off-color pop up and they drag him in to get his brains kicked out because he had a record. Sure, he put in three semesters in the college on the Hudson, and he wasn't too anxious to do anything that would put him in his senior year where it took a lifetime to matriculate. Ever since he wrangled that chauffeur's job from Rudolph York I hadn't heard from him . . . until now, after York's little genius of a son had been snatched.

Rain started to spatter against the windshield when I turned into the drive. The headlights picked out the roadway and I followed it up to the house. Every light in the place was on as if the occupants were afraid a dark corner might conceal some unseen terror.

It was a big place, a product of wealth and good engineering, but in spite of its stately appearance and wrought-iron gates, somebody had managed to sneak in, grab the kid and beat it. Hell, the kid was perfect snatch bait. He was more than a son to his father, he was the result of a fourteen-year experiment. Then, that's what he got for bringing the kid up to be a genius. I bet he'd shell out plenty of his millions to see him safe and sound.

The front door was answered by one of those tailored flunkies who must always count up to fifty before they open up. He gave me a curt nod and allowed me to come in out of the rain anyway.

"I'm Mike Hammer," I said, handing him a card. "I'd like to see your boss. And right away," I added.

The flunky barely glanced at the pasteboard. "I'm awfully sorry, sir, but Mr. York is temporarily indisposed."

When I shoved a cigarette in my mouth and lit it I said, "You tell him it's about his kid. He'll un-indispose himself in a hurry."

I guess I might as well have told him I wanted a ransom payment right then the way he looked at me. I've been taken for a lot of things in my life, but this was the first for a snatch artist. He started to stutter, swallowed, then waved his hand in the general direction of the living room. I followed him in.

Have you ever seen a pack of alley cats all set for a midnight brawl when something interrupts them? They spin on a dime with the hair still up their backs and watch the intruder through hostile eye slits as though they were ready to tear him so they could continue their own fight. An intense, watchful stare of mutual hate and fear.

That's what I ran into, only instead of cats it was people. Their expressions were the same. A few had been sitting, others stopped their quiet pacing and stood poised, ready. A tableau of hate. I looked at them only long enough to make a mental count of a round dozen and tab them as a group of ghouls whose morals had been eaten into by dry rot a long time.

Rudolph York was slumped in a chair gazing blankly into an empty fireplace. The photos in the rags always showed him to be a big man, but he was small and tired-looking this night. He kept muttering to himself, but I couldn't hear him. The butler handed him my card. He took it, not bothering to look at it.

"A Mr. Hammer, sir."

No answer.

"It . . . It's about Master Ruston, sir."

Rudolph York came to life. His head jerked around and he looked at me with eyes that spat fire. Very slowly he came to his feet, his hands trembling. "Have you got him?"

Two boys who might have been good-looking if it weren't for the nightclub pallor and the squeegy skin came out of a settee together. One had his fists balled up, the other plunked his highball glass on a coffee table. They came at me together. Saps. All I had to do was look over my shoulder and let them see what was on my face and they called it quits outside of swinging distance.

I turned my attention back to Rudolph York. "No."

"Then what do you want?"

"Look at my card."

He read, "Michael Hammer, Private Investigator," very slowly, then crushed the card in his hand. The contortions in his face were weird. He breathed silent, unspeakable words through tight lips, afraid to let himself be heard. One look at the butler and the flunky withdrew quietly, then he turned back to me. "How did you find out about this?" he charged.

I didn't like this guy. As brilliant a scientist as he might be, as wealthy and important, I still didn't like him. I blew a cloud of smoke in his direction. "Not hard," I answered, "not hard at all. I got a telephone call."

He kept beating his fist into an open palm. "I don't want the police involved, do you hear! This is a private matter."

"Cool off, doc. I'm not the police. However, If you try to keep me out of this I'll buzz one of the papers, then your privacy will really be shot to hell."

"Whom do you represent?" he asked coldly.

"Your chauffeur, Billy Parks."

"So?"

"So I'd like to know why you put the finger on him when you found out your kid was missing. I'd like to know why you let them mangle him without a formal charge even being lodged, and why you're keeping all this under your hat. And by damn you better start speaking and pretty loud at that!"

"Please, Mr. Hammer."

A hand hit my shoulder and spun me, another came up from the side and cracked across my face. The punk said, "How dare you talk to Uncle like that!"

I let him get it out then backhanded him across the mouth with all I had. This time the other one

14

grabbed my coat. He got a short jab in the ribs that bent him over, then the palm of my hand across his puss that straightened him up again. I shoved him away and got the punk's tie in my hand. When I was breathing in his face I twisted on the tie until the blue started running up his neck, then I smacked him on each side of that whisky-sodden face until my hand hurt. When I dropped him he lay on the floor crying, trying to cover his face with his hands.

I spoke to the general assembly rather than to him. "In case anyone else has ideas like that, he'd better have more in his hands than a whisky glass."

York hadn't missed a trick. He looked old again. The fire left his eyes and he groped for the arm of his chair. York was having a pretty rough time of it, but after having seen Billy I didn't feel sorry for him.

I threw my butt in the fireplace and parked in the chair opposite him. He didn't need any prompting. "Ruston was not in his bed in the morning. It had been slept in, but he was not there. We searched the house and the grounds for him, but found no trace of his presence. I must have become excited. The first thing that entered my head was that I had an ex-convict in my employ. I called the local police and reported what had taken place. They led Parks away. I've since regretted the incident."

"I imagine," I remarked dryly. "How much is it costing you to keep this quiet?"

He shuddered. "Nothing. I did offer them a re-

15

ward if they could locate Ruston."

"Oh, swell. Great. That's all they needed. Cripes, you got a brain like a fly!" His eyes widened at that. "These local jokers aren't cops. Sure, they'd be quiet, who wouldn't? Do you think they'd split the kind of reward money you'd be offering if they could help it?"

I felt like rapping him in the teeth. "Throwing Billy to the wolves was stupid. Suppose he was an ex-con. With three convictions to his credit he wasn't likely to stick his neck out for that offence. He'd be the first suspect as it was. Damn, I'd angle for Dilwick before I would Billy. He's more the type."

York was sweating freely. He buried his face in his hands and swayed from side to side, moaning to himself. He stopped finally, then looked up at me. "What will I do, Mr. Hammer? What *can* be done?"

I shook my head.

"But something must be done! I must find Ruston. After all these years . . . I can't call the police. He's such a sensitive boy . . . I — I'm afraid."

"I merely represent Billy Parks, Mr. York. He called me because he was in a jam and I'm his friend. What I want from you is to give him back his job. Either that or I call the papers."

"All right. It really doesn't matter." His head dropped again. I put on my hat and stood up, then, "But you? Mr. Hammer, you aren't the police as you say. Perhaps you could help me, too."

I threw him a straw. "Perhaps."

He grabbed at it. "Would you? I need somebody . . . who will keep this matter silent."

"It'll cost you."

"Very well, how much?"

"How much did you offer Dilwick?"

"Ten thousand dollars."

I let out a whistle, then told him, "Okay, ten G's plus expenses."

Relief flooded his face like sunlight. The price was plenty steep but he didn't bat an eye. He had been holding this inside himself too long and was glad to hand it to someone else.

But he still had something to say. "You drive a hard bargain, Mr. Hammer, and in my position I am forced, more or less, to accept. However, for my own satisfaction I would like to know one thing, how good a detective are you?"

He said it in a brittle tone and I answered him the same way. An answer that made him pull back away from me as though I had a contagious disease. I said, "York, I've killed a lot of men. I shot the guts out of two of them in Times Square. Once I let six hundred people in a nightclub see what some crook had for dinner when he tried to gun me. He got it with a steak knife. I remember because I don't want to remember. They were too nasty. I hate the bastards that make society a thing to be laughed at and preyed upon. I hate them so much I can kill without the slightest compunction. The papers call me dirty names and the kind of rats I monkey with are scared stiff of me, but

17

I don't give a damn. When I kill I make it legal. The courts accuse me of being too quick on the trigger but they can't revoke my license because I do it right. I think fast, I shoot fast, I've been shot at plenty. And I'm still alive. That's how good a detective I am."

For a full ten seconds he stood speechless, staring at me with an undisguised horror. There wasn't a sound from the room. It isn't often that I make a speech like that, but when I do it must be convincing. If thoughts could be heard that house would be a babble of fearful confusion. The two punks I biffed looked like they had just missed being bitten by a snake. York was the first one to compose himself. "I suppose you'd like to see the boy's room?"

"Uh-uh."

"Why not? I thought . . ."

"The kid's gone, that's enough. Seeing the room won't do any good. I don't have the equipment to fool around with clues, York. Fingerprints and stuff are for technical men. I deal with motives and people."

"But the motive . . ."

I shrugged. "Money, probably. That's what it usually is. Let's start at the beginning first." I indicated the chair and York settled back. I drew up closer to him. "When did you discover him to be missing?"

"Yesterday morning. At eight o'clock, his regular rising hour, Miss Malcom, his governess, went into his room. He was not in bed. She looked for him throughout the house, then told me he could not be found. With the aid of the gardener and Parks we searched the grounds. He was not there."

"I see. What about the gatekeeper?"

"Henry saw nothing, heard nothing."

"Then you called the police, I suppose?" He nodded. "Why did you think he was kidnapped?"

York gave an involuntary start. "But what other reason could account for his disappearance?"

I leaned forward in my seat. "According to all I've ever read about your son, Mr. York, he is the most brilliant thing this side of heaven. Wouldn't a young genius be inclined to be highly strung?"

He gripped the arms of the chair until the veins stood out on the back of his hands. The fire was in his eyes again. "If you are referring to his mental health, you are mistaken. Ruston was in excellent spirits as he has been all his life. Besides being his father and a scientist, I am also a doctor."

It was easy to see that he didn't want any doubts cast upon the mind of one he had conditioned so carefully so long. I let it go for the time being.

"Okay, describe him to me. Everything. I have to start somewhere."

"Yes. He is fourteen. In appearance he is quite like other boys. By appearance I mean expressions, manners and attitudes. He is five feet one-inch tall, light brown hair, ruddy complexion. He weighs one hundred twelve pounds stripped. Eyes, brown, slight scar high on the left side of his forehead as the result of a fall when he was younger."

"Got a picture of him?" The scientist nodded, reached inside his jacket pocket and came out with a snapshot. I took it. The boy was evidently standing in the yard, hands behind his back in a typically shy-youth manner. He was a good-looking kid at that. A slight smile played around his mouth and he seemed to be pretty self-conscious. He had on shorts and a dark sweater. Romping in the background was a spotted spaniel.

"Mind if I keep it?" I asked.

York waved his hand. "Not at all. If you want them, there are others."

When I pocketed the snap I lit another cigarette. "Who else is in the house? Give me all the servants, where they sleep, anyone who has been here recently. Friends, enemies, people you work with."

"Of course." He cleared his throat and listed the household. "Besides myself, there is Miss Malcom, Parks, Henry, two cooks, two maids and Harvey. Miss Grange works for me as a laboratory assistant, but lives at home in town. As for friends, I have few left that I ever see since I stopped teaching at the university. No enemies I can think of. I believe the only ones who have been inside the gate the past few weeks were tradesmen from town. That is," he indicated the gang in the room with a thumb, "outside these, my closest relatives. They are here and gone constantly."

"You are quite wealthy?" The question was unnecessary, but I made my point.

York cast a quick look about him, then a grimace that was half disgust passed over him. "Yes, but my health is still good."

I let the ghouls hear it. "Too bad for them."

"The servants all sleep in the north wing. Miss Malcom has a room adjoining Ruston's and connected to it. I occupy a combination study and bedroom at the front of the house.

"I work with no one and for no one. The nature of my work you must be familiar with; it is that of giving my son a mind capable of greater thought and intelligence than is normally found. He may be a genius to you and others, but to me he is merely one who makes full use of his mind. Naturally, my methods are closely guarded secrets. Miss Grange shares them with me, but I trust her completely. She is as devoted to my son as I am. Since the death of my wife when the child was born, she has aided me in every way. I think that is all?"

"Yeah, I guess that'll do."

"May I ask how you will proceed?"

"Sure. Until we get a sign from whoever kidnapped your son I'm going to sit tight. The ones that grabbed the kid must think they know what they're doing, otherwise they wouldn't pick someone like your boy who is always in the public eye. If you wanted to you could have every cop in the state beating the bushes. I take it there was no note . . ."

"None at all."

". . . so they're playing it close to see what you'll do. Call the cops and they're liable to take a powder. Hold off a bit and they will contact you. Then

I'll go to work . . . that is if it's really a snatch."

He bit into his lip and gave me another of those fierce looks. "You say that as though you don't think he was kidnapped."

"I say that because I don't *know* he was kidnapped. It could be anything. I'll tell you better when I see a ransom note."

York didn't get a chance to answer, for at that moment the butler reappeared, and between him and the luscious redhead they supported a bloody, limp figure. "It's Parks, sir. Miss Malcom and I found him outside the door!"

We ran to him together. York gasped when he saw Parks' face then sent the butler scurrying off for some hot water and bandages. Most of the gore had been wiped off, but the swellings were as large as ever. The desk sergeant had done as I told him, the hour wasn't up yet, but somebody was still going to pay for this. I carried Billy to a chair and sat him down gently.

I stepped back and let York go to work when the butler returned with a first-aid kit. It was the first good chance I had to give Miss Malcom the once-over all the way from a beautiful set of legs through a lot of natural curves to an extraordinarily pretty face. Miss Malcom they called her.

I call her Roxy Coulter. She used to be a strip artist in the flesh circuit of New York and Miami.

Chapter Two

But Roxy had missed her profession. Hollywood should have had her. Maybe she didn't remember Atlantic City or that New Year's Eve party in Charlie Drew's apartment. If she did she held a dandy deadpan and all I got in return for my stare was one of those go ahead peeks, but don't touch looks.

A peek was all I got, because Billy came around with a groan and made an effort to sit up. York put his hand against his chest and forced him down again. "You'll have to be quiet," he cautioned him in a professional tone.

"My face," his eyes rolled in his head, "jeez, what happened to my face?"

I knelt beside him and turned over the cold compress on his forehead. His eyes gleamed when he recognized me. "Hello, Mike. What happened?"

"Hi, Billy. They beat up on you. Feel any better?"

"I feel awful. Oh, that bastard. If only I was bigger, Mike . . . damn, why couldn't I be big like you? That dirty . . ."

"Forget about him, kid." I patted his shoulder. "I handed him a little of the same dish. His map'll

23

never be the same."

"Cripes! I bet you did! I thought something funny happened down there. Thanks, Mike, thanks a lot."

"Sure."

Then his face froze in a frightened grimace. "Suppose . . . suppose they come back again? Mike . . . I — I can't stand that stuff. I'll talk, I'll say anything. I can't take it, Mike!"

"Ease off. I'm not going anywhere. I'll be around."

Billy tried to smile and he gripped my arm. "You will?"

"Yup. I'm working for your boss now."

"Mr. Hammer." York was making motions from the side of the room. I walked over to him. "It would be better if he didn't get too excited. I gave him a sedative and he should sleep. Do you think you can manage to carry him to his room? Miss Malcom will show you the way."

"Certainly," I nodded. "And if you don't mind, I'd like to do a little prowling afterward. Maybe question the servants."

"Of course. The house is at your disposal."

Billy's eyes had closed and his head had fallen on his chin when I picked him up. He'd had a rough time of it all right. Without a word Miss Malcom indicated that I was to follow her and led me through an arch at the end of the room. After passing through a library, a study and a trophy room that looked like something out of a museum, we wound up in a kitchen. Billy's room was off an alcove behind the pantry. As gently as I could I laid him under the covers. He was sound asleep.

Then I stood up. "Okay, Roxy, now we can say hello."

"Hello, Mike."

"Now why the disguise and the new handle? Hiding out?"

"Not at all. The handle as you call it is my real name. Roxy was something I used on the stage."

"Really? Don't tell me you gave up the stage to be a diaper changer. What are you doing here?"

"I don't like your tone, Mike. You change it or go to hell."

This was something. The Roxy I knew never had enough self-respect to throw her pride in my face. Might as well play it her way.

"Okay, baby, don't get teed off on me. I have a right to be just a little bit curious, haven't I? It isn't very often that you catch somebody jumping as far out of character as you have. Does the old man know about the old life?"

"Don't be silly. He'd can me if he did."

"I guessed as much. How did you tie up in this place?"

"Easy. When I finally got wise to the fact that I was getting my brains knocked out in the big city I went to an agency and signed up as a registered nurse. I was one before I got talked into tossing my torso around for two hundred a week. Three days later Mr. York accepted me to take care of his child. That was two years ago. Anything else you want to know?"

I grinned at her. "Nope. It was just funny meeting you, that's all."

"Then may I leave?"

I let my grin fade and eased her out through the door. "Look, Roxy, is there somewhere we can go talk?"

"I don't play those games anymore, Mike."

"Get off my back, will you? I mean talk."

She arched her eyebrows and watched me steadily a second, then seeing that I meant it, said, "My room. We can be alone there. But only talk, remember?"

"Roger, bunny, let's go."

This time we went into the outer foyer and up a stairway that seemed to have been carved out of a solid piece of mahogany. We turned left on the landing and Roxy opened the door for me.

"In here," she said.

While I picked out a comfortable chair she turned on a table lamp then offered me a smoke from a gold box. I took one and lit it. "Nice place you got here."

"Thank you. It's quite comfortable. Mr. York sees that I have every convenience. Now shall we talk?"

She was making sure I got the point in a hurry. "The kid. What is he like?"

Roxy smiled a little bit, and the last traces of hardness left her face. She looked almost maternal. "He's wonderful. A charming boy."

"You seem to like him."

"I do. You'd like him too." She paused, then, "Mike . . . do you really think he was kidnapped?"

"I don't know, that's why I want to talk about him. Downstairs I suggested that he might have become temporarily unbalanced and the old man nearly chewed my head off. Hell, it isn't unreasonable to figure that. He's supposed to be a genius and that automatically puts him out of the normal class. What do you think?"

She tossed her hair back and rubbed her forehead with one hand. "I can't understand it. His room is next door, and I heard nothing although I'm usually a light sleeper. Ruston was perfectly all right up to then. He wouldn't simply walk out."

"No? And why not?"

"Because he is an intelligent boy. He likes everyone, is satisfied with his environment and has been very happy all the time I've known him."

"Uh-huh. What about his training? How did he get to be a genius?"

"That you'll have to find out from Mr. York. Both he and Miss Grange take care of that department."

I squashed the butt into the ashtray. "Nuts, it doesn't seem likely that a genius can be made. They have to be born. You've been around him a lot. Tell me, just how much of a genius is he? I know only what the papers print."

"Then you know all I know. It isn't what he knows that makes him a genius, it's what he is capable of learning. In one week he mastered every phase of the violin. The next week it was the piano.

Oh, I realize that it seems impossible, but it's quite true. Even the music critics accept him as a master of several instruments. It doesn't stop there, either. Once he showed an interest in astronomy. A few days later he exhausted every book on the subject. His father and I took him to the observatory where he proceeded to amaze the experts with his uncanny knowledge. He's a mathematical wizard besides. It doesn't take him a second to give you the cube root of a six-figure number to three decimal points. What more can I say? There is no field that he doesn't excel in. He grasps fundamentals at the snap of the fingers and learns in five minutes what would take you or me years of study. That, Mike, is the genius in a nutshell, but that's omitting the true boy part of him. In all respects he is exactly like other boys."

"The old man said that too."

"He's quite right. Ruston loves games, toys and books. He has a pony, a bicycle, skates and a sled. We go for long walks around the estate every once in a while and do nothing but talk. If he wanted to he could expound on nuclear physics in ten-syllable words, but that isn't his nature. He'd sooner talk football."

I picked another cigarette out of the box and flicked a match with my thumbnail. "That about covers it, I guess. Maybe he didn't go off his nut at that. Let's take a look at his room."

Roxy nodded and stood up. She walked to the end of the room and opened a door. "This is it." When she clicked on the light switch I walked in. I don't know what I expected, but this wasn't it. There were pennants on the walls and pictures tucked into the corners of the dresser mirror. Clothes were scattered in typical boyish confusion over the backs of chairs and the desk.

In one corner was the bed. The covers had been thrown to the foot and the pillow still bore the head print of its occupant. If the kid had really been snatched I felt for him. It was no night to be out in your pajamas, especially when you left the top of them hanging on the bedpost.

I tried the window. It gave easily enough, though it was evident from the dust on the outside of the sill that it hadn't been opened recently.

"Keep the kid's door locked at night?" I asked Roxy.

She shook her head. "No. There's no reason to."

"Notice any tracks around here, outside the door or window?"

Another negative. "If there were any," she added, "they would have been wiped out in the excitement."

I dragged slowly on the cigarette, letting all the facts sink in. It seemed simple enough, but was it? "Who are all the twerps downstairs, bunny?"

"Relatives, mostly."

"Know 'em?"

Roxy nodded. "Mr. York's sister and her husband, their son and daughter, and a cousin are his only blood relations. The rest are his wife's folks. They've been hanging around here as long as I've been here, just waiting for something to happen to York."

"Does he know it?"

"I imagine so, but he doesn't seem bothered by them. They try to outdo each other to get in the old boy's favor. I suppose there's a will involved. There usually is."

"Yeah, but they're going to have a long wait. York told me his health was perfect."

Roxy looked at me curiously, then dropped her eyes. She fidgeted with her fingernails a moment and I let her stew a bit before I spoke.

"Say it, kid."

"Say what?"

"What you have on your mind and almost said."

She bit her lip, hesitating, then, "This is between you and me, Mike. If Mr. York knew I told you this I'd be out of a job. You won't mention it, will you?"

"I promise."

"About the second week I was here I happened to overhear Mr. York and his doctor after an examination. Apparently Mr. York knew what had happened, but called in another doctor to verify it. For some time he had been working with special apparatus in his laboratory and in some way became over exposed to radiation. It was enough to cause some internal complications and shorten his life-span. Of course, he isn't in any immediate danger of dying, but you never can tell. He wasn't burned seriously, yet considering his age, and the fact that his injury has had a chance to work on

30

him for two years, there's a possibility that any emotional or physical excitement could be fatal."

"Now isn't that nice," I said. "Do you get what that means, Roxy?" She shook her head. "It might mean that somebody else knows that too and tried to stir the old boy up by kidnapping the one closest to him in the hope that he kicks off during the fun. Great . . . that's a nice subtle sort of murder."

"But that's throwing it right on the doorstep of the beneficiary of his estate."

"Is it? I bet even a minor beneficiary would get enough of the long green to make murder worthwhile. York has plenty."

"There are other angles too, Mike."

"Been giving it some thought, haven't you?" I grinned at her. "For instance, one of the family might locate the kid and thus become number-one boy to the old man. Or perhaps the kid was the chief beneficiary and one of them wanted to eliminate him to push himself further up the list. Yeah, kid, there's a lot of angles, and I don't like any of 'em."

"It still might be a plain kidnapping."

"Roger. That it might. It's just that there're a lot more possibilities to it that could make it interesting. We'll know soon enough." I opened the door and hesitated, looking over my shoulder. " 'Night, Roxy."

"Good night."

York was back by the fireplace again, still brooding. I would have felt better if he had been pacing the floor. I walked over and threw myself in a big chair. "Where'll I spend the night?" I asked him.

He turned very slowly. "The guest room. I'll ring for Harvey."

"Never mind. I'll get him myself when I'm ready."

We sat in silence a few minutes then York began a nervous tapping of his fingers. Finally, "When do you think we'll have word?"

"Two, three days maybe. Never can tell."

"But he's been gone a day already."

"Tomorrow, then. I don't know."

"Perhaps I should call the police again."

"Go ahead, but you'll probably be burying the boy after they find him. Those punks aren't cops, they're political appointees. You ought to know these small towns. They couldn't find their way out of a paper bag."

For the first time he showed a little parental anxiety. His fist came down on the arm of the chair. "Damn it, man, I can't simply sit here! What do you think it's like for me? Waiting. Waiting. He may be dead now for all we know."

"Perhaps, but I don't think so. Kidnapping's one thing, murder's another. How about introducing me to those people?"

He nodded. "Very well." Every eye in the room was on me as we made the rounds. I didn't suppose there would be anyone too anxious to meet me after the demonstration a little while ago.

The two gladiators were first. They were sitting on the love seat trying not to look shaky. Both of them still had red welts across their cheeks. The introduction was simple enough. York merely pointed in obvious disdain. "My nephews, Arthur and William Graham."

We moved on. "My niece, Alice Nichols." A pair of deep brown eyes kissed mine so hard I nearly lost my balance. She swept them up and down the full length of me. It couldn't have been any better if she did it with a wet paintbrush. She was tall and she had seen thirty, but she saw it with a face and body that were as fresh as a new daisy. Her clothes made no attempt at concealment; they barely covered. On some people skin is skin, but on her it was an invitation to dine. She told me things with a smile that most girls since Eve have been trying to put into words without being obvious or seeming too eager and I gave her my answer the same way. I can run the ball a little myself.

York's sister and her husband were next. She was a middle-aged woman with "Matron" written all over her. The type that wants to entertain visiting dignitaries and look down at "peepul" through a lorgnette. Her husband was the type you'd find paired off with such a specimen. He was short and bulgy in the middle. His single-breasted gray suit didn't quite manage to cross the equator without putting a strain on the button. He might have had hair, but you'd never know it now. One point of his collar had jumped the tab and stuck out like an accusing finger.

York said, "My sister, Martha Ghent, her husband, Richard." Richard went to stick out his hand but the old biddie shot him a hasty frown and he drew back, then she tried to freeze me out. Failing in this she turned to York. "Really, Rudolph, I hardly think we should meet this . . . this person."

York turned an appealing look my way, in apology. "I'm sorry, Martha, but Mr. Hammer considers it necessary."

"Nevertheless, I don't see why the police can't handle this."

I sneered at her in my finest manner. "I can't see why you don't keep your mouth shut, Mrs. Ghent."

The way her husband tried to keep the smile back, I thought he'd split a gut. Martha stammered, turned blue and stalked off. York looked at me critically, though approvingly.

A young kid in his early twenties came walking up as though the carpet was made of eggs. He had Ghent in his features, but strictly on his mother's side. A pipe stuck out of his pocket and he sported a set of thick-lensed glasses. The girl at his side didn't resemble anyone, but seeing the way she put her arm around Richard I took it that she was the daughter.

She was. Her name was Rhoda, she was friendly and smiled. The boy was Richard, Junior. He raised his eyebrows until they drew his eyes over the rims of his glasses and peered at me disapprovingly. He perched his hands on his hips and "Humphed" at me. One push and he would be over the line that divides a man and a pansy.

The introductions over, I cornered York out of earshot of the others. "Under the circumstances, it might be best if you kept this gang here until things settle down a bit. Think you can put them up?"

"I imagine so. I've been doing it at one time or another for the last ten years. I'll see Harvey and have the rooms made up."

"When you get them placed, have Harvey bring me a diagram showing where their rooms are. And tell him to keep it under his hat. I want to be able to reach anyone anytime. Now, is there anyone closely connected with the household we've missed?"

He thought a moment. "Oh, Miss Grange. She went home this afternoon."

"Where was she during the kidnapping?"

"Why . . . at home, I suppose. She leaves here between five and six every evening. She is a very reserved woman. Apparently has very little social activity. Generally she furthers her studies in the library rather than go out anywhere."

"Okay, I'll get to her. How about the others? Have they alibis?"

"Alibis?"

"Just checking, York. Do you know where they were the night before last?"

"All . . . I can't speak for all of them, but Arthur and William were here. Alice Nichols came in about nine o'clock then left about an hour later."

This part I jotted down on a pad. "How did

you collect the family . . . or did they all just drift in?"

"No, I called them. They helped me search, although it did no good. Mr. Hammer, what are we going to do? Please . . ."

Very slowly, York was starting to go to pieces. He'd stood up under this too calmly too long. His face was pale and withered-looking, drawn into a mask of tragedy.

"First of all, you're going to bed. It won't do any good for you to be knocking yourself out. That's what I'm here for." I reached over his shoulder and pulled a velvet cord. The flunky came in immediately and hurried over to us. "Take him upstairs," I said.

York gave the butler instructions about putting the family up and Harvey seemed a little surprised and pleased that he'd be allowed in on the conspiracy of the room diagram.

I walked to the middle of the floor and let the funeral buzz down before speaking. I wasn't nice about it. "You're all staying here tonight. If it interferes with other plans you've made it's too bad. Anyone that tries to duck out will answer to me. Harvey will give you your rooms and be sure you stay in them. That's all."

Lady sex appeal waited until I finished then edged up to me with a grin. "See if you can grab the end bedroom in the north wing," she said, "and I'll get the one connected to it."

I said in mock surprise, "Alice, you can get hurt doing things like that."

She laughed. "Oh, I bruise easily, but I heal fast as hell."

Swell girl. I hadn't been seduced in a long time.

I wormed out through a cross fire of nasty looks to the foyer and winked at Richard Ghent on the way. He winked back; his wife wasn't looking.

I slung on my coat and hat and went out to the car. When I rolled it through the gate I turned toward town and stepped on the gas. When I picked up to seventy I held it there until I hit the main drag. Just before the city line I pulled up to a gas station and swung in front of a pump. An attendant in his early twenties came out of the miniature Swiss Alpine cottage that served as a service station and automatically began unscrewing the gas cap. "Put in five," I told him.

He snaked out the hose and shoved the nose in the tank, watching the gauge. "Open all night?" I quizzed.

"Yeah."

"On duty yourself?"

"Yup. 'Cept on Sundays."

"Don't suppose you get much to do at night around here."

"Not very much."

This guy was as talkative as a pea pod. "Say, was much traffic along here night before last?"

He shut off the pump, put the cap back on and looked at me coldly. "Mister, I don't know from nothing," he said.

It didn't take me long to catch on to that remark. I handed him a ten-spot and followed him inside while he changed it. I let go a flyer. "So the cops kind of hinted that somebody would be nosing around, huh?"

No answer. He rang the cash register and began counting out bills. "Er . . . did you happen to notice Dilwick's puss? Or was it one of the others?"

He glanced at me sharply, curiously. "It was Dilwick. I saw his face."

Instead of replying I held out my right hand. He peered at it and saw where the skin had been peeled back off half the knuckles. This time I got a great big grin.

"Did you do that?"

"Uh-huh."

"Okay, pal, for that we're buddies. What do you want to know?"

"About traffic along here night before last."

"Sure, I remember it. Between nine o'clock and dawn the next morning about a dozen cars went past. See, I know most of 'em. A couple was from out of town. All but two belonged to the up-country farmers making milk runs to the separator at the other end of town."

"What about the other two?"

"One was a Caddy. I seen it around a few times. Remember it because it had one side dented in. The other was that Grange dame's two-door sedan. Guess she was out wolfing." He laughed at that.

"Grange?"

"Yeah, the old bag that works out at York's place. She's a stiff one."

"Thanks for the info, kid." I slipped him a buck and he grinned. "By the way, did you pass that on to the cops too?"

"Not me. I wouldn't give them the right time."

"Why?"

"Lousy bunch of bastards." He explained it in a nutshell without going into detail.

I hopped in and started up, but before I drove off I stuck my head out the window. "Where's this Grange babe live?"

"At the Glenwood Apartments. You can't miss it. It's the only apartment house in this burg."

Well, it wouldn't hurt to drop up and see her anyway. Maybe she had been on her way home from work. I gunned the engine and got back on the main drag, driving slowly past the shaded fronts of the stores. Just outside the business section a large green canopy extended from the curb to the marquee of a modern three-story building. Across the side in small, neat letters was GLEN-WOOD APARTMENTS. I crawled in behind a black Ford sedan and hopped out.

Grange, Myra, was the second name down. I pushed the bell and waited for the buzzer to unlatch the door. When it didn't come I pushed it again. This time there was a series of clicks and I shoved the door open. One flight of stairs put me in front of her apartment. Before I could ring, the metal peephole was pulled back and a pair of dark eyes threw insults at me.

"Miss Grange?"

"Yes."

"I'd like to speak to you if you can spare a few moments."

"Very well, go ahead." Her voice sounded as if it came out of a tree trunk. This made the third person I didn't like in Sidon.

"I work for York," I explained patiently, "I'd like to speak to you about the boy."

"There's nothing I care to discuss."

Why is it that some dames can work me up into a lather so fast with so little is beyond me, but this one did. I quit playing around. I pulled out the .45 and let her get a good look at it. "You open that door or I'll shoot the lock off," I said.

She opened it. The insults in her eyes turned to terror until I put the rod back under cover. Then I looked at her. If she was an old bag I was Queen of the May. Almost as tall as I was, nice brown hair cut short enough to be nearly mannish and a figure that seemed to be well molded, except that I couldn't tell too well because she was wearing slacks and a house jacket. Maybe she was thirty, maybe forty. Her face had a built-in lack of expression like an old painting. Wearing no makeup didn't help it any, but it didn't hurt, either.

I tossed my hat on a side table and went inside without being invited. Myra Grange followed me closely, letting her wooden-clad sandals drag along the carpet. It was a nice dump, but small. There was something to it that didn't sit right, as though the choice of furniture didn't fit her personality. Hell, maybe she just sublet.

The living room was ultramodern. The chairs and the couch were surrealist dreams of squares and angles. Even the coffee table was balanced precariously on little pyramids that served as legs. Two framed wood nymphs seemed cold in their nudity against the background of the chilled blue walls. I wouldn't live in a room like this for anything.

Myra held her position in the middle of the floor, legs spread, hands shoved in her side pockets. I picked a leather-covered ottoman and sat down.

She watched every move I made with eyes that scarcely concealed her rage. "Now that you've forced your way in here," she said between tight lips, "perhaps you'll explain why, or do I call the police?"

"I don't think the police would bother me much, kiddo." I pulled my badge from my pocket and let her see it. "I'm a private dick myself."

"Go on." She was a cool tomato.

"My name is Hammer. Mike Hammer. York wants me to find the kid. What do you think happened?"

"I believe he was kidnapped, Mr. Hammer. Surely that is evident."

"Nothing's evident. You were seen on the road fairly late the night the boy disappeared. Why?"

Instead of answering me she said, "I didn't think the time of his disappearance was established."

"As far as I'm concerned it is. It happened that night. Where were you?"

She began to raise herself up and down on her

toes like a British major. "I was right here. If anyone said he saw me that night he was mistaken."

"I don't think he was." I watched her intently. "He's got sharp eyes."

"He was mistaken," she repeated.

"All right, we'll let it drop there. What time did you leave York's house?"

"Six o'clock, as usual. I came straight home." She began to kick at the rug impatiently, then pulled a cigarette from a pocket and stuck it in her mouth. Damn it, every time she moved she did something that was familiar to me but I couldn't place it. When she lit the cigarette she sat down on the couch and watched me some more.

"Let's quit the cat and mouse, Miss Grange. York said you were like a mother to the kid and I should suppose you'd like to see him safe. I'm only trying to do what I can to locate him."

"Then don't classify me as a suspect, Mr. Hammer."

"It's strictly temporary. You're a suspect until you alibi yourself satisfactorily then I won't have to waste my time and yours fooling around."

"Am I alibied?"

"Sure," I lied. "Now can you answer some questions civilly?"

"Ask them."

"Number one. Suspicious characters loitering about the house anytime preceding the disappearance."

She thought a moment, furrowing her eyebrows. "None that I can recall. Then again, I am inside

42

all day working in the lab. I wouldn't see anyone."

"York's enemies. Do you know them?"

"Rudolph . . . Mr. York has no enemies I know of. Certain persons working in the same field have expressed what you might call professional jealousy, but that is all."

"To what extent?"

She leaned back against the cushions and blew a smoke ring at the ceiling. "Oh, the usual bantering at the clubs. Making light of his work. You know."

I didn't know anything of the kind, but I nodded. "Anything serious?"

"Nothing that would incite a kidnapping. There were heated discussions, yes, but few and far between. Mr. York was loathe to discuss his work. Besides, a scientist is not a person who would resort to violence."

"That's on the outside. Let's hear a little bit about his family. You've been connected with York long enough to pick up a little something on his relatives."

"I'd rather not discuss them, Mr. Hammer. They are none of my affair."

"Don't be cute. We're talking about a kidnapping."

"I still don't see where they could possibly enter into it."

"Damn it," I exploded, "you're not supposed to. I want information and everybody wants to play repartee. Before long I'm going to start choking it out of people like you."

"Please, Mr. Hammer, that isn't necessary."

"So I've been told. Then give."

"I've met the family very often. I know nothing about them although they all try to press me for details of our work. I've told them nothing. Needless to say, I like none of them. Perhaps that is a biased opinion but it is my only one."

"Do they feel the same toward you?"

"I imagine they are very jealous of anyone so closely connected with Mr. York as I am," she answered with a caustic grimace. "You might surmise that of any rich man's relatives. However, for your information and unknown to them, I enjoy a personal income outside the salary Mr. York pays me and I am quite unconcerned with the disposition of his fortune in the event that anything should happen to him. The only possession he has that I am interested in is the boy. I have been with him all his life, and as you say, he is like a son to me. Is there anything else?"

"Just what is York's work . . . and yours?"

"If he hasn't told you, I'm not at liberty to. Naturally, you realize that it centered around the child."

"Naturally." I stood up and looked at my watch. It was nine-fifteen. "I think that covers it, Miss Grange. Sorry to set you on your ear to get in, but maybe I can make it up some time. What do you do nights around here?"

Her eyebrows went up and she smiled for the first time. It was more of a stifled laugh than a smile and I had the silly feeling that the joke was

44

on me. "Nothing you'd care to do with me," she said.

I got sore again and didn't know why. I fought a battle with the look, stuck my hat on and got out of there. Behind me I heard a muffled chuckle.

The first thing I did was make a quick trip back to the filling station. I waited until a car pulled out then drove up to the door. The kid recognized me and waved. "Any luck?" he grinned.

"Yeah, I saw her. Thought she was an old bag?"

"Well, she's a stuffy thing. Hardly ever speaks."

"Listen," I said, "are you sure you saw her the other night?"

"Natch, why?"

"She said no. Think hard now. Did you see her or the car?"

"Well, it was her car. I know that. She's the only one that ever drives it."

"How would you know it?"

"The aerial. It's got a bend in it so it can only be telescoped down halfway. Been like that ever since she got the heap."

"Then you can't be certain she was in it. You wouldn't swear to it?"

"Well . . . no. Guess not when you put it that way. But it was her car," he insisted.

"Thanks a lot." I shoved another buck at him. "Forget I was around, will you?"

"Never saw you in my life," he grinned. Nice kid.

This time I took off rather aimlessly. It was only to pacify York that I left the house in the first place. The rain had let up and I shut off the windshield wipers while I turned onto the highway and cruised north toward the estate. If the snatch ran true to form there would be a letter or a call sometime soon. All I could do would be to advise York to follow through to get the kid back again then go after the ones that had him.

If it weren't for York's damn craving for secrecy I could buzz the state police and have a seven-state alarm sent out, but that meant the house would crawl with cops. Let a spotter get a load of that and they'd dump the kid and that'd be the end of it until some campers came across his remains sometime. As long as the local police had a sizable reward to shoot for they wouldn't let it slip. Not after York told them not to.

I wasn't underestimating Dilwick any. I'd bet my bottom dollar he'd had York's lines tapped already, ready to go to town the moment a call came through. Unless I got that call at the same time I was liable to get scratched. Not me, brother. Ten G's was a lot of mazuma in any language.

The lights were still on en masse when I breezed by the estate. It was still too early to go back, and as long as I could keep the old boy happy by doing a little snooping I figured I was earning my keep, at least. About ten miles down the highway the town of Bayview squatted along the water's edge waiting for summer to liven things up.

A kidnap car could have gone in either direction, although this route was unlikely. Outside Bayview the highway petered off into a tar road that completely disappeared under drifting winter sands. Anything was worth trying, though. I dodged an old flivver that was standing in the middle of the road and swerved into the gravel parking place of a two-bit honky-tonk. The place was badly run down at the heels and sadly in need of a paint job. A good deodorant would have helped, too. I no sooner got my foot on the rail when a frowsy blonde sidled up to me and I got a quick once-over. "You're new around here ain't you?"

"Just passing through."

"Through to where? That road outside winds up in the drink."

"Maybe that's where I'm going."

"Aw now, Buster, that ain't no way to feel. We all got our troubles but you don't wanna do nothing like that. Lemme buy you a drink, it'll make you feel better."

She whistled through her teeth and when that got no response, cupped her hands and yelled to the bartender who was busy shooting crap on the bar. "Hey, Andy, get your tail over here and serve your customers."

Andy took his time. "What'll you have, pal?"

"Beer."

"Me too."

"You too nothing. Beat it, Janie, you had too much already."

"Say, see here, I can pay my own way."

"Not in my joint."

I grinned at the two of them and chimed in.

"Give her a beer why don't you?"

"Listen, pal, you don't know her. She's half tanked already. One more and she'll be making like a Copa cutie. Not that I don't like the Copa, but the dames there are one thing and she's another, just like night and day. Instead of watching, my customers all get the dry heaves and trot down to Charlie's on the waterfront."

"Well, I like that!" Janie hit an indignant pose and waved her finger in Andy's face. "You give me my beer right now or I'll make better'n the Copa. I'll make like . . . like . . . ."

"Okay, okay, Janie, one more and that's all."

The bartender drew two beers, took my dough instead of Janie's and rang it up. I put mine away in one gulp. Janie never reached completely around her glass. Before Andy could pick out the change Janie had spilled hers halfway down the bar.

Andy said something under his breath, took the glass away then fished around under the counter for a rag. He started to mop up the mess.

I watched. In my head the little bells were going off, slowly at first like chimes on a cold night. They got louder and louder, playing another scrambled, soundless symphony. A muscle in my neck twitched. I could almost feel that ten grand in my pocket already. Very deliberately I reached out across the bar and gathered a handful of Andy's stained apron in my fist. With my other hand I yanked out the .45 and held it an inch away from his eye. He was staring death in the face and knew it.

I had trouble keeping my voice down. "Where did you get that bar rag, Andy?"

His eyes shifted to the blue-striped pajama bottoms that he held in his hand, beer soaked now, but recognizable. The other half to them were in Ruston York's bedroom hanging on the foot of the bed.

Janie's mouth was open to scream. I pointed the gun at her and said, "Shut up." The scream died before it was born. She held the edge of the bar with both hands, shaking like a leaf. Ours was a play offstage; no one saw it, no one cared: "Where, Andy?"

". . . Don't know, mister. Honest . . ."

I thumbed the hammer back. He saw me do it. "Only one more chance, Andy. Think hard."

His breath came in little jerks; fright thickened his tongue. "Some . . . guy. He brought it in. Wanted to know . . . if they were mine. It . . . was supposed to be a joke. Honest, I just use it for a bar rag, that's all."

"When?"

". . .'s afternoon."

"Who. Andy?"

"Bill. Bill Cuddy. He's a claim digger. Lives in a shack on the bay."

I put the safety back on, but I still held his apron. "Andy," I told him, "if you're leveling with me it's okay, but if you're not, I'm going to shoot your head off. You know that, don't you?"

His eyes rolled in his head then came back to

49

meet mine. "Yeah, mister. I know. I'm not kidding. Honest, I got two kids . . ."

"And Janie here. I think maybe you better keep her with you for a while. I wouldn't want anyone to hear about this, understand?"

Andy understood, all right. He didn't miss a word. I let him go and he had to hang on to his bar to keep from crumbling. I slid the rod back under my coat, wrung out the pajamas and folded them into a square.

When I straightened my hat and tie I said, "Where is Cuddy's place?"

Andy's voice was so weak I could hardly hear it. "Straight . . . down the road to the water. Turn left. It's the deck . . . deckhouse of an old boat pulled up on the . . . beach."

I left them standing there like Hansel and Gretel in the woods, scared right down to their toes. Poor Andy. He didn't have anymore to do with it than I did, but in this game it's best not to take any chances.

As Janie had said, the road led right to the drink. I parked the car beside a boarded-up house and waded through the wet sand on foot. Ten feet from the water I turned left and faced a line of broken-down shacks that were rudely constructed from the junk that comes in on the tide. Some of them had tin roofs, with the advertisements for soft drinks and hot dogs still showing through.

Every once in a while the moon would shine through a rift in the clouds, and I took advantage of it to get a better look at the homemade village.

Cuddy's place was easier to find than I expected. It was the only dump that ever had seen paint, and on the south side hung a ship's name plate with CARMINE spelled out in large block letters. It was a deckhouse, all right, probably washed off during a storm. I edged up to a window and looked in. All I could see were a few vague outlines. I tried the door. It opened outward noiselessly. From one corner of the room came the raspy snore of a back-sleeper with a load under his belt.

A match lit the place up. Cuddy never moved, even when I put the match to the ship's lantern swinging from the center of the ceiling. It was a one-room affair with a few chairs, a table and a double-decker bed along the side. He had rigged up a kerosene stove with the pipe shooting through the roof and used two wooden crates for a larder. Beside the stove was a barrel of clams.

Lots of stuff, but no kid.

Bill Cuddy was a hard man to awaken. He twitched a few times, pawed the covers and grunted. When I shook him some more his eyelids flickered, went up. No pupils. They came down ten seconds later. A pair of bleary, bloodshot eyes moved separately until they came to an accidental focus on me.

Bill sat up. "Who're you?"

I gave him a few seconds to study me, then palmed my badge in front of his face. "Cop. Get up."

His legs swung to the floor, he grabbed my arm. "What's the matter, officer? I ain't been poachin'.

All I got is clams, go look." He pointed to the barrel. "See?"

"I'm no game warden," I told him.

"Then whatcha want of me?"

"I want you for kidnapping. Murder maybe."

"Oh . . . No!" His voice was a hoarse croak. "But . . . I ain't killed nobody atall. I wouldn't do that."

He didn't have to tell me that. There are types that kill and he wasn't one of them. I didn't let him know I thought so.

"You brought a set of pajamas into Andy's place this afternoon. Where did you get them?"

He wrinkled his nose, trying to understand what I was talking about. "Pajamas?"

"You heard me."

He remembered then. His face relaxed into a relieved grin. "Oh, that. Sure, I found 'em lying on Shore Road. Thought I'd kid Andy with 'em."

"You almost kidded him to death. Put on your pants. I want you to show me the spot."

He stuck his feet into a pair of dungarees and pulled the suspenders over his bony shoulders, then dragged a pair of boots out from under the bed. A faded denim shirt and a battered hat and he was dressed. He kept shooting me sidewise glances, trying to figure it out but wasn't getting anyplace.

"You won't throw me in the jug, will you?"

"Not if you tell the truth."

"But I did."

"We'll see. Come on." I let him lead the way.

The sand had drifted too deep along the road to take the car so we plodded along slowly, keeping away from the other shacks. Shore Road was a road in name only. It was a strip of wet Sahara that separated the tree line from the water. A hundred yards up and the shacks had more room between them. Bill Cuddy pointed ahead.

"Up there is the cove where I bring the boat in. I was coming down there and where the old cistern is I see the pants lying right in the middle of the road."

I nodded. A few minutes later we had reached the cistern, a huge, barrel-shaped thing lying on its side. It was big enough to make a two-car garage. Evidently it, like everything else around here, had been picked up during a storm and deposited along the shore. Bill indicated a spot on the ground with a gnarled forefinger.

"Right here's the spot, officer, they was lying right here."

"Fine. See anyone?"

"Naw. Who would be out here? They was washed up, I guess."

I looked at him, then the water. Although the tide was high the water was a good forty yards from the spot. He saw what I meant and he shifted uneasily.

"Maybe they blew up."

"Bill?"

"Huh?"

"Did you ever see wet clothes blow along the ground? Dry clothes, maybe, but wet?"

He paused. "Nope."

"Then they didn't blow up or wash up. Somebody dropped them there."

He got jittery then, his face was worried. "But I didn't do it. No kidding. I just found them there. They was new-looking so I brung 'em to Andy's. You won't jug me, will you? I . . ."

"Forget it, Bill. I believe you. If you want to keep your nose clean turn around and trot home. Remember this, though. Keep your mouth shut, you hear?"

"Gee, yeah. Thanks . . . thanks, officer. I won't say nothing to nobody." Bill broke into a fast shuffle and disappeared into the night.

Alone like that you can see that what you mistook for silence was really a jungle of undertones, subdued, foreign, but distinct. The wind whispering over the sand, the waves keeping time with a steady lap, lap. Tree sounds, for which there is no word to describe bark rubbing against bark, and the things that lived in the trees. The watch on my wrist made an audible tick.

Somewhere oars dipped into the water and scraped in the oarlocks. There was no telling how far away it was. Sounds over water carry far on the wind.

I tried to see into the night, wondering how the pajamas got there. A road that came from the cove and went nowhere. The trees and the bay. A couple of shacks and a cistern.

The open end faced away from me, making it necessary to push through yards of saw grass to reach it. Two rats ran out making ugly squeaking noises. When I lit a match I seemed to be in a hall of green slime. Droplets of water ran down the curved sides of the cistern and collected in a stinking pool of scum in the middle. Some papers had blown in, but that was all. The only things that left their footprints in the muck had tails. When I couldn't hold my breath any longer I backed out and followed the path I had made to the road.

Right back where I started. Twenty-five yards away was the remains of a shack. The roof had fallen in, the sides bulged out like it had been squeezed by a giant hand. Further down was another. I took the first one. The closer I came to it the worse it looked. Holes in the side passed for windows, the door hung open on one hinge and was wedged that way by a pile of sand that had blown around the corner. No tracks, no nothing. It was as empty as the cistern.

Or so I thought.

Just then someone whimpered inside. The .45 leaped into my hand. I took a few wooden matches, lit them all together and threw them inside and went in after them.

I didn't need my gun. Ruston York was all alone, trussed up like a Christmas turkey over in the corner, his naked body covered with bruises.

In a moment I was on my knees beside him, working the knots loose. I took it easy on the adhesive tape that covered his mouth so I wouldn't tear the skin off. His body shook with sobs. Tears of fright and relief filled his large, expressive eyes, and when he had his arms free he threw them around my neck. "Go ahead and cry, kid," I said.

He did, then. Hard, body-racking gasps that must have hurt. I wiggled out of my jacket and put it around him, talking quickly and low to comfort him. The poor kid was a mess.

It came with jarring suddenness, that sound. I shoved the kid on his back and pivoted on my heels. I was shooting before I completed the turn. Someone let out a short scream. A heavy body crashed into my chest and slammed my back against the wall. I kicked out with both feet and we spilled to the floor. Before I could get my gun up a heavy boot ripped it out of my hand.

They were all over me. I gave it everything I had, feet, fingernails and teeth, there wasn't enough room to swing. Somehow I managed to hook my first two fingers in a mouth and yank, and I felt a cheek rip clear to the ear.

There was no more for me. Something smashed down on my skull and I stopped fighting. It was a peaceful feeling, as if I were completely adrift from my body. Feet thudded into my ribs and pounded my back raw, but there was no pain, merely vague impressions. Then even the impressions began to fade.

Chapter Three

I came back together like a squadron of flak-eaten bombers re-forming. I heard the din of their motors, a deafening, pulsating roar that grew louder and louder. Pieces of their skin, fragments of their armor drifted to earth and imbedded themselves in my flesh until I thought I was on fire.

Bombs thudded into the earth and threw great flashes of flame into my face and rocked my body back and forth, back and forth. I opened my eyes with an effort.

It was the kid shaking me. "Mister. Can you get up? They all ran away looking for me. If you don't get up they'll be back and find us. Hurry, please hurry."

I tried to stand up, but I didn't do too good a job. Ruston York got his arms around me and boosted. Between the two of us I got my feet in position where I could shove with my legs and raise myself. He still had on my coat, but that was all.

I patted his shoulder. "Thanks, kid. Thanks a lot."

It was enough for a while. He steered me outside and up into the bushes along the trees where we melted into the darkness. The sand muffled our footsteps well. For once I was grateful for the steady drip of rain from the trees; it covered any other noises we made.

"I found your gun on the floor. Here, do you want it?" He held the .45 out gingerly by the handle. I took it in a shaking hand and stowed it in the holster. "I think you shot somebody. There's an awful lot of blood by the door."

"Maybe it's mine," I grunted.

"No, I don't think so. It's on the wall, too, and there's a big hole in the wall where it looks like a bullet went through."

I prayed that he was right. Right now I half-hoped they'd show again so I could have a chance to really place a few where they'd hurt.

I don't know how long it took to reach the car, but it seemed like hours. Every once in a while I thought I could discern shouts and guarded words of caution. By the time Ruston helped slide me under the wheel I felt as though I had been on the Death March.

We sat there in silence a few moments while I fumbled for a cigarette. The first drag was worth a million dollars. "There's a robe in the back," I told the kid. He knelt on the seat, got it and draped it over his legs.

"What happened?"

"Gosh, mister, I hardly know. When you pushed me away I ran out the door. The man I think you shot nearly grabbed me, but he didn't. I hid behind the door for a while. They must have thought I ran off because when they followed me out one man told the others to scatter and search the beach, then he went away too. That's when I came in and got you."

I turned the key and reached for the starter. It hurt. "Before that. What happened then?"

"You mean the other night?"

"Yeah."

"Well, I woke up when the door opened. I thought maybe it was Miss Malcom. She always looks in before she goes to bed, but it wasn't her. It was a man. I wanted to ask him who he was when he hit me. Right here." Ruston rubbed the top of his head and winced.

"Which door did he come in?"

"The one off the hall, I think. I was pretty sleepy."

Cute. Someone sneaks past the guard at the gate, through a houseful of people and puts the slug on the kid and walks off with him.

"Go on." While he spoke I let in the clutch and swung around, then headed the car toward the estate.

"I woke up in a boat. They had me in a little room and the door was locked. I could hear the men talking in the stern and one called the man who was steering, Mallory. That's the only time I heard a name at all."

The name didn't strike any responsive chord as far as I was concerned, so I let him continue.

"Then I picked the lock and . . ."

"Wait a second, son." I looked at him hard. "Say that again."

"I picked the lock. Why?"

"Just like that you picked the lock. No trouble to it or anything?"

"Uh-uh." He flashed a boyish grin at me, shyly. "I learned all about locks when I was little. This one was just a plain lock."

He *must* be a genius. It takes me an hour with respectable burglar tools to open a closet door.

". . . and as soon as I got out I opened a little hatch and crawled up on the deck, I saw the lights from shore and jumped overboard. Boy, was that water cold. They never even heard me at all. I nearly made it at that. After I jumped the boat kept right on going and disappeared, but I guess they found the door open down below. I should have locked it again but I was sort of scared and forgot. Just when I got up on the shore some man came running at me and they had me again. He said he'd figured I'd head for the lights, then he slapped me. He was waiting for the others to come and he made me go into the shack with him. Seems like they tied up in the cove and had to wait awhile before they could take me back to the boat.

"He had a bottle and started drinking from it, and pretty soon he was almost asleep. I waited until he was sort of dopey then threw my pajama pants out the window with a rock in them hoping someone would find them. He never noticed what I did. But he did know he was getting drunk, and he didn't have any more in the bottle. He hit me a few times and I tried to get away. Then he really gave it to me. When he got done he took some rope and tied me up and went down the beach after the others. That was when you came in."

"And I went out," I added.

"Gee, mister, I hope you didn't get hurt too badly." His face was anxious, truly anxious. It's been a long time since someone worried about me getting hurt. I ran my fingers through his hair and shook his head gently.

"It isn't too bad, kid," I said. He grinned again, pulled the robe tighter and moved closer to me. Every few seconds he'd throw me a searching glance, half curious, half serious.

"What's your name?"

"Mike Hammer."

"Why do you carry a gun?"

"I'm a detective, Ruston. A private detective."

A sigh of relief escaped him. He probably figured me for one of the mob who didn't like the game, I guess.

"How did you happen to find me?"

"I was looking for you."

"I'm . . . I'm glad it was you, Mr. Hammer, and not somebody else. I don't think anyone would have been brave enough to do what you did."

I laughed at that. He was a good kid. If any bravery was involved he had it all. Coming back in after me took plenty of nerve. I told him so, but he chuckled and blushed. Damn, you couldn't help but like him. In spite of a face full of bruises and all the hell he had been through he could still smile. He sat there beside me completely at ease, watching me out of the corner of his eye as though

I was a tin god or something.

For a change some of the lights were off in the house. Henry, the gatekeeper, poked a flashlight in the car and his mouth fell open. All he got out was, "M . . . Master Ruston!"

"Yeah, it's him. Open the gates." He pulled a bar at the side and the iron grillwork rolled back. I pushed the buggy through, but by the time I reached the house Henry's call had the whole family waiting on the porch.

York didn't even wait until I stopped. He yanked the door open and reached for his son. Ruston's arms went around his neck and he kept repeating, "Dad . . . Dad."

I wormed out of the car and limped around to the other side. The family was shooting questions at the kid a mile a minute and completely ignored me, not that it mattered. I shoved them aside and took York by the arm. "Get the kid in the house and away from this mob. He's had enough excitement for a while."

The scientist nodded. Ruston said, "I can walk, Dad." He held the robe around himself and we went in together.

Before the others could follow, York turned. "If you don't mind, please go to your rooms. You will hear what happened in the morning."

There was no disputing who was master in that house. They looked at one another then slouched off in a huff. I drew a few nasty looks myself.

I slammed the door on the whole pack of them and started for the living room, but Harvey interrupted me en route. Having once disrupted his composure, events weren't likely to do it a second time. When he handed me the tray with the diagram of the bedroom layout neatly worked up he was the perfect flunky.

"The guest plan, sir," he said. "I trust it is satisfactory?"

I took it without looking at it and thanked him, then stuck it in my pocket.

York was in an anteroom with his son. The kid was stretched out on a table while his father went over each bruise carefully, searching for abrasions. Those he daubed with antiseptic and applied small bandages. This done he began a thorough examination in the most professional manner.

When he finished I asked, "How is he?"

"All right, apparently," he answered, "but it will be difficult to tell for a few days. I'm going to put him to bed now. His physical condition has always been wonderful, thank goodness."

He wrapped Ruston in a robe and rang for Harvey. I picked up the wreckage that was my coat and slipped into it. The butler came in and at York's direction, picked the kid up and they left the room. On the way out Ruston smiled a goodnight at me over the butler's shoulder.

York was back in five minutes. Without a word he pointed at the table and I climbed on. By the time he finished with me I felt like I had been in a battle all over again. The open cuts on my face and back stung from iodine, and with a few layers of six-inch tape around my ribs I could hardly breathe. He told me to get up in a voice shaky from suppressed emotion, swallowed a tablet from a bottle in his kit and sat down in a cold sweat.

When I finished getting dressed I said, "Don't you think you ought to climb into the sack yourself? It's nearly daybreak." He shook his head. "No. I want to hear about it. Everything. Please, if you don't mind . . . the living room."

We went in and sat down together. While I ran over the story he poured me a stiff shot of brandy and I put it away neat.

"I don't understand it. Mr. Hammer . . . it is beyond me."

"I know. It doesn't seem civilized, does it?"

"Hardly." He got up and walked over to a Sheraton secretary, opened it and took out a book. He wrote briefly and returned waving ten thousand dollars in my face. "Your fee, Mr. Hammer. I scarcely need say how grateful I am."

I tried not to look too eager when I took that check, but ten G's is ten G's. As unconcernedly as I could, I shoved it in my wallet. "Of course, I suppose you want me to put a report in to the state police," I remarked. "They ought to be able to tie into that crew, especially with the boat. A thing like that can't be hidden very easily."

"Yes, yes, they will have to be apprehended. I can't imagine why they chose to abduct Ruston. It's incredible."

"You are rich, Mr. York. That is the primary reason."

64

"Yes. Wealth does bring disadvantages sometimes, though I have tried to guard against it."

I stood up. "I'll call them then. We have one lead that might mean something. One of the kidnappers was called Mallory. Your boy brought that up."

"What did you say?"

I repeated it.

His voice was barely audible. "Mallory . . . No!"

As if in a trance he hurried to the side of the fireplace. A pressure on some concealed spring-activated hidden mechanism and the side swung outward. He thrust his hand into the opening. Even at this distance I could see him pale. He withdrew his hand empty. A muscular spasm racked his body. He pressed his hands against his chest and sagged forward. I ran over and eased him into a chair.

"Vest . . . pocket."

I poked my fingers under his coat and brought out a small envelope of capsules. York picked one out with trembling fingers and put it on his tongue. He swallowed it, stared blankly at the wall. Very slowly a line of muscles along his jaw hardened into knots, his lips curled back in an animal-like snarl. "The bitch," he said, "the dirty man-hating bitch has sold me out."

"Who, Mr. York? Who was it?"

He suddenly became aware of me standing there. The snarl faded. A hunted-quarry look replaced it. "I said nothing, you understand? Nothing."

I dropped my hand from his shoulder. I was

starting to get a dirty taste in my mouth again. "Go to hell," I said, "I'm going to report it."

"You wouldn't dare!"

"Wouldn't I? York, old boy, that son of yours pulled me out of a nasty mess. I like him. You hear that? I like him more than I do a lot of people. If you want to expose him to more danger that's your affair, but I'm not going to have it."

"No . . . that's not it. This can't be made public."

"Listen, York, why don't you stow that publicity stuff and think of your kid for a change? Keep this under your hat and you'll invite another snatch and maybe you won't be so lucky. Especially," I added, "since somebody in your household has sold you out."

York shuddered from head to foot.

"Who was it, York? Who's got the bull on you?"

"I . . . have nothing to say."

"No? Who else knows you're counting your hours because of those radiation burns? What's going to happen to the kid when you kick off?"

That did it. He turned a sick color. "How did you find out about that?"

"It doesn't matter. If I know it others probably do. You still didn't tell me who's putting the squeeze on you."

"Sit down, Mr. Hammer. Please."

I pulled up a chair and parked.

"Could I," he began, "retain you as sort of a guardian instead of reporting this incident? It would be much simpler for me. You see, there are certain scientific aspects of my son's training that you, as a layman, would not understand, but if brought to light under the merciless scrutiny of the newspapers and a police investigation might completely ruin the chances of a successful result.

"I'm not asking you to understand, I'm merely asking that you cooperate. You will be well paid, I assure you. I realize that my son is in danger, but it will be better if we can repel any danger rather than prevent it at its source. Will you do this for me?"

Very deliberately I leaned back in my chair and thought it over. Something stunk. It smelled like Rudolph York. But I still owed the kid a debt.

"I'll take it, York, but if there's going to be trouble I'd like to know where it will come from. Who's the man-hating turnip that has you in a brace?"

His lips tightened. "I'm afraid I cannot reveal that, either. You need not do any investigating. Simply protect my interests, and my son."

"Okay," I said as I rose. "Have it your own way. I'll play dummy. But right now I'm going to beat the sheet. It's been a tough day. You'd better hit it yourself."

"I'll call Harvey."

"Never mind, I'll find it." I walked out. In the foyer I pulled the diagram out of my pocket and checked it. The directions were clear enough. I went upstairs, turned left at the landing and followed the hand-carved balustrade to the other side. My room was next to last and my name was on white cardboard, neatly typed, and framed in a small brass holder on the door. I turned the knob, reached for the light and flicked it on.

"You took long enough getting here."

I grinned. I wondered what Alice Nichols had used as a bribe to get Harvey to put me in next to her. "Hello, kitten."

Alice smiled through a cloud of smoke. "You were better-looking the last time I saw you."

"So? Do I need a shave?"

"You need a new face. But I'll take you like you are." She shrugged her shoulders and the spider web of a negligee fell down to her waist. What she had on under it wasn't worth mentioning. It looked like spun moonbeams with a weave as big as chicken wire. "Let's go to bed."

"Scram, kitten. Get back in your own hive."

"That's a corny line, Mike, don't play hard to get."

I started to climb out of my clothes. "It's not a line, kitten, I'm beat."

"Not that much."

I draped my shirt and pants over the back of the chair and flopped in the sack. Alice stood up slowly. No, that's not the word. It was more like a low-pressure spring unwinding. The negligee was all the way off now. She was a concert of savage beauty.

"Still tired?"

"Turn off the light when you go out, honey." Before I rolled over she gave me a malicious grin. It told me that there were other nights. The lights went out. Before I corked off one thought hit me.

It couldn't have been Alice Nichols he had meant when he called some babe a man-hating bitch.

Going to sleep with a thought like that is a funny thing. It sticks with you. I could see Alice over and over again, getting up out of that chair and walking across the room, only this time she didn't even wear moonbeams. Her body was lithe, seductive. She did a little dance. Then someone else came into my dream, too. Another dame. This one was familiar, but I couldn't place her. She did a dance too, but a different kind. There was none of that animal grace, no fluid motion. She took off her clothes and moved about stiffly, ill at ease. The two of them started dancing together, stark naked, and this new one was leading. They came closer, the mist about their faces parted and I got a fleeting glimpse of the one I couldn't see before.

I sat bolt upright in bed. No wonder Miss Grange did things that bothered me. It wasn't the woman I recognized in her apartment, it was her motions. Even to striking a match toward her the way a man would. Sure, she'd be a man-hater, why not? She was a Lesbian.

"Damn!"

I hopped out of bed and climbed into my pants. I picked out York's room from the diagram and tiptoed to the other side of the house. His door was partly opened. I tapped gently. No answer.

I went in and felt for the switch. Light flooded the room, but it didn't do me any good. York's bed had never been slept in. One drawer of his

69

desk was half-open and the contents pushed aside. I looked at the oil blot on the bottom of the drawer. I didn't need a second look at the hastily opened box of .32 cartridges to tell me what had been in there. York was out to do murder.

Time, time, there wasn't enough of it. I finished dressing on the way out. If anyone heard the door slam after me or the motor start up they didn't care much. No lights came on at all. I slowed up by the gates, but they were gaping open. From inside the house I could hear a steady snore. Henry was a fine gatekeeper.

I didn't know how much of a lead he had. Sometime hours ago my watch had stopped and I didn't reset it. It could have been too long ago. The night was fast fading away. I don't think I had been in bed a full hour.

On that race to town I didn't pass a car. The lights of the kid's filling station showed briefly and swept by. The unlit head lamps of parked cars glared in the reflection of my own brights and went back to sleep.

I pulled in behind a line of cars outside the Glenwood Apartments. Switched off the engine and climbed out. There wasn't a sign of life anywhere. When this town went to bed it did a good job.

It was one time I couldn't ring doorbells to get in. If Ruston had been with me it wouldn't have taken so long; the set of skeleton keys I had didn't come up with the right answer until I tried two dozen of them.

The .45 was in my fist. I flicked the safety off

70

as I ran up the stairs. Miss Grange's door was closed, but it wasn't locked; it gave when I turned the knob.

No light flared out the door when I kicked it open. No sound broke the funeral quiet of the hall. I stepped in and eased the door shut behind me.

Very slowly I bent down and unlaced my shoes, then put them beside the wall. There was no sense sending in an invitation. With my hand I felt along the wall until I came to the end of the hall. A switch was to the right. Cautiously, I reached around and threw it up, ready for anything.

I needn't have been so quiet. Nobody would have yelled. I found York, all right. He sat there grinning at me like a blooming idiot with the top of his head holding up a meat cleaver.

Chapter Four

Now it was murder. First it was kidnapping, then murder. There seems to be no end to crime. It starts off as a little thing, then gets bigger and bigger like an over-inflated tire until it busts all to hell and gone.

I looked at him, the blood running red on his face, seeping out under the clots, dripping from the back of his head to the floor. It was only a guess, but I figured I had been about ten minutes too late.

The room was a mess, a topsy-turvy cell of ripped-up furniture and emptied drawers. The carpet was littered with trash and stuffing from the pillows. York still clutched a handful of papers, sitting there on the floor where he had fallen, staring blankly at the wall. If he had found what he was searching for it wasn't here now. The papers in his hand were only old receipted electric bills made out to Myra Grange.

First I went back and got my shoes, then I picked up the phone. "Give me the state police," I told the operator.

A Sergeant Price answered. I gave it to him briefly. "This is Mike Hammer, Sergeant," I said.

"There's been a murder at the Glenwood Apartments and as far as I can tell it's only a few minutes old. You'd better check the highways. Look for a Ford two-door sedan with a bent radio antenna. Belongs to a woman named Myra Grange. Guy that's been bumped is Rudolph York. She works for him. Around thirty, I'd say, five, six or seven, short hair, well built. Not a bad-looking tomato. No, I don't know what she was wearing. Yeah . . . yeah, I'll stay here. You want me to inform the city cops?" The sergeant said some nasty things about the city boys and told me to go ahead.

I did. The news must have jarred the guy on the desk awake because he started yelling his fool head off all over the place. When he asked for more information I told him to come look for himself, grinned into the mouthpiece and hung up.

I had to figure this thing out. Maybe I could have let it go right then, but I didn't think that way. My client was dead, true, but he had overpaid me in the first place. I could still render him a little service gratis.

I checked the other rooms, but they were as scrambled as the first one. Nothing was in place anywhere. I had to step over piles of clothes in the bedroom that had been carefully, though hurriedly, turned inside out.

The kitchen was the only room not torn apart. The reason for that was easy to see. Dishes and pans crashing against the floor would bring someone running. Here York had felt around, moved articles, but not swept them clear of the shelves.

A dumbwaiter door was built into the wall. It was closed and locked. I left it that way. The killer couldn't have left by that exit and still locked it behind him, not with a hook-and-clasp. I opened the drawers and peered inside. The fourth one turned up something I hadn't expected to see. A meat cleaver.

That's one piece of cutlery that is rarely duplicated in a small apartment. In fact, it's more or less outdated. Now there were two of them.

The question was: Who did York surprise in this room? No, it wasn't logical. Rather, who surprised York? It had to be that way. If York had burst in here on Grange there would have been a scene, but at least she would have been here too. It was hard picturing her stepping out to let York smash up the joint.

When York came in the place was empty. He came to kill, but finding his intended victim gone, forgot his primary purpose and began his search. Kill. Kill. That was it. I looked at the body again. What I looked for wasn't there anymore.

Somebody had swiped the dead man's gun.

Why? Damn these murderers anyway, why must they mess things up so? Why the hell can't they just kill and be done with it? York sat there grinning for all he was worth, defying me to find the answer. I said, "Cut it out, pal. I'm on your side."

Two cleavers and a grinning dead man. Two cleavers, one in the kitchen and one in his head. What kind of a killer would use a cleaver? It's too big to put in a pocket, too heavy to swing properly unless you had a fairly decent wrist. It would have to be a man, no dame likes to kill when there's a chance of getting spattered with blood.

But Myra Grange . . . the almost woman. She was more half man. Perhaps her sensibilities wouldn't object to crunching a skull or getting smeared with gore. But where the hell did the cleaver come from?

York grinned. I grinned back. It was falling into place now. Not the motive, but the action of the crime, and something akin to motive. The killer knew York was on his way here and knew Grange was out. The killer carried the cleaver for several reasons. It might have just been handy. Having aimed and swung it was certain to do the job. It was a weapon to which no definite personality could be attached.

Above all things, it was far from being an accidental murder. I hate premeditation. I hate those little thoughts of evil that are suppressed in the mind and are being constantly superimposed upon by other thoughts of even greater evil until they squeeze out over the top and drive a person to the depths of infamy.

And this murder was premeditated. Perhaps that cleaver was supposed to have come from the kitchen, but no one could have gone past York to the kitchen without his seeing him, and York had a gun. The killer had chosen his weapon, followed York here and caught him in the act of rifling the place. He didn't even have to be silent

75

about it. In the confusion of tearing the place apart York would never have noticed little sounds . . . until it was too late.

The old man half-stooping over the desk, the upraised meat-ax, one stroke and it was over. Not even a hard stroke. With all that potential energy in a three-pound piece of razor-sharp steel, not much force was needed to deliver a killing blow. Instantaneous death, the body twisting as it fell to face the door and grin at the killer.

I got no further. There was a stamping in the hall, the door was pushed open and Dilwick came in like a summer storm. He didn't waste any time. He walked up to me and stood three inches away, breathing hard. He wasn't pretty to look at.

"I ought to kill you, Hammer," he grated.

We stood there in that tableau a moment. "Why don't you?"

"Maybe I will. The slightest excuse, any excuse. Nobody's going to pull that on me and get away with it. Not you or anybody."

I sneered at him. "Whenever you're ready, Dilwick, here or in the mayor's office, I don't care."

Dilwick would have liked to have said more, but a young giant in the gray and brown leather of the state police strode over to me with his hand out. "You Mike Hammer?" I nodded.

"Sergeant Price," he smiled. "I'm one of your fans. I had occasion to work with Captain Chambers in New York one time and he spent most of the time talking you up."

The lad gave me a bone-crushing handshake that was good to feel.

I indicated the body. "Here's your case, Sergeant."

Dilwick wasn't to be ignored like that. "Since when do the state police have jurisdiction over us?"

Price was nice about it. "Ever since you proved yourselves to be inadequately supplied with material . . . and men." Dilwick flushed with rage. Price continued, addressing his remarks to me. "Nearly a year ago the people of Sidon petitioned the state to assist in all police matters when the town in general and the county in particular was being used as a rendezvous and sporting place by a lot of out-of-state gamblers and crooks."

The state cop stripped off his leather gloves and took out a pad. He noted a general description of the place, time, then asked me for a statement. Dilwick focused his glare on me, letting every word sink in.

"Mr. York seemed extremely disturbed after his son had been returned to him. He . . ."

"One moment, Mr. Hammer. Where was his son?"

"He had been kidnapped."

"So?" Price's reply was querulous. "It was never reported to us."

"It was reported to the city police." I jerked my thumb at Dilwick. "He can tell you that."

Price didn't doubt me, he was looking for

Dilwick's reaction. "Is this true?"

"Yes."

"Why didn't we hear about it?"

Dilwick almost blew his top. "Because we didn't feel like telling you, that's why." He took a step nearer Price, his fists clenched, but the state trooper never budged. "York wanted it kept quiet and that's the way we handled it, so what?"

It came back to me again. "Who found the boy?"

"I did." Dilwick was closer to apoplexy than ever. I guess he wanted that ten grand as badly as I did. "Earlier this evening I found the boy in an abandoned shack near the waterfront. I brought him home. Mr. York decided to keep me handy in case another attempt was made to abduct the kid."

Dilwick butted in. "How did you know York was here?"

"I didn't." I hated to answer him, but he was still the police. "I just thought he might be. The boy had been kicked around and I figured that he wanted Miss Grange in the house."

The fat cop sneered. "Isn't York big enough to go out alone anymore?"

"Not in his condition. He had an attack of some sort earlier in the evening."

Price said, "How did you find out he was gone, Mr. Hammer?"

"Before I went to sleep I decided to look in to see how he was. He hadn't gone to bed. I knew he'd mentioned Miss Grange and, as I said, figured he had come here."

Price nodded. "The door . . . ?"

"It was open. I came in and found . . . this." I swept my hand around. "I called you, then the city police. That's all."

Dilwick made a face and bared what was left of his front teeth. "It stinks."

So it did, but I was the only one who was sure of it.

"Couldn't it have been like this, Mr. Hammer." Dilwick emphasized the *mister* sarcastically. "You find the kid, York doesn't like to pay out ten thousand for hardly any work, he blows after you threaten him, only you followed him and make good the threat."

"Sure, it could," I said, "except that it wasn't." I poked a butt in my mouth and held a match to it. "When I kill people I don't have to use a meat hatchet. If they got a gun, I use a gun. If they don't I use my mitts." I shifted my eyes to the body. "I could kill him with my fingers. On bigger guys . . . I'd use both hands. But no cleaver."

"How did York get here, Mr. Hammer?"

"Drove, I imagine. You better detail a couple of boys to lock up his car. A blue '64 Caddy sedan."

Price called a man in plain clothes over with his forefinger and repeated the instructions. The guy nodded and left.

The coroner decided that it was time to get there with the photo guys and the wicker basket. For ten minutes they went around dusting the place and snapping flashes of the remains from all positions until they ran out of bulbs. I showed Price where I'd touched the wall and the switch so there wouldn't be a confusion of the prints. For the record he asked me if I'd give him a set of impressions. It was all right with me. He took out a cardboard over which had been spread a light paraffin of some sort and I laid both hands on it and pressed. Price wrote my name on the bottom, took the number off my license and stowed it back in his pocket.

Dilwick was busy going through the papers York had scattered about, but finding nothing of importance returned his attention to the body. The coroner had spread the contents of the pockets out on an end table and Price rifled through them. I watched over his shoulder. Just the usual junk: a key ring, some small change, a wallet with two twenties and four tens and membership cards in several organizations. Under the wallet was the envelope with the capsules.

"Anything missing?" Price asked.

I shook my head. "Not that I know of, but then, I never went through his pockets."

The body was stuffed into a wicker basket, the cleaver wrapped in a towel and the coroner left with his boys. More troopers came in with a few city guys tagging along and I had to repeat my story all over again. Standing outside the crowd was a lone newspaperman, writing like fury in a note pad. If this was New York they'd have to bar the doors to hold back the press. Just wait until the story reached the wires. This town wouldn't be able to hold them all.

Price called me over to him. "You'll be where I'll be able to reach you?"

"Yeah, at York's estate."

"Good enough. I'll be out sometime this morning."

"I'll be with him," Dilwick cut in. "You keep your nose out of things, too, understand?"

"Blow it," I said. "I know my legal rights."

I shoved my hat on and stamped my butt out in an ashtray. There was nothing for me here. I walked to the door, but before I could leave Price hurried after me. "Mr. Hammer."

"Yeah, Sergeant?"

"Will I be able to expect some cooperation from you?"

I broke out a smile. "You mean, if I uncover anything will I let you in on it, don't you?"

"That covers it pretty well." He was quite serious.

"Okay," I agreed, "but on one condition."

"Name it."

"If I come across something that demands immediate action, I'm going to go ahead on it. You can have it too as soon as I can get it to you, but I won't sacrifice a chance to follow a lead to put it in your hands."

He thought a moment, then, "That sounds fair enough. You realize, of course, that this isn't a permit to do as you choose. The reason I'm willing to let you help out is because of your reputation. You've been in this racket longer than I have, you've had the benefit of wide experience and are familiar with New York police methods. I know your history, otherwise you'd be shut out of this case entirely. Shorthanded as we are, I'm personally glad to have you help out."

"Thanks, Sergeant. If I can help, I will. But you'd better not let Dilwick get wise. He'd do anything to stymie you if he heard about this."

"That pig," Price grunted. "Tell me, what are you going to do?"

"The same thing you are. See what became of the Grange dame. She seems to be the key figure right now. You putting out a dragnet?"

"When you called, a roadblock was thrown across the highways. A seven-state alarm is on the Teletype this minute. She won't get far. Do you know anything of her personally?"

"Only that she's supposed to be the quiet type. York told me that she frequents the library a lot, but I doubt if you'll find her there. I'll see what I can pick up at the house. If I latch on to anything about her I'll buzz you."

I said so long and went downstairs. Right now the most important thing in my life was getting some sleep. I felt like I hadn't seen a pillow in months. A pair of young troopers leaned against the fender of a blue Caddy sedan parked down further from my heap. They were comparing notes and talking back and forth. I'd better remind Billy to come get it.

The sun was thumbing its nose at the night when I reached the estate. Early-morning trucks that the gas station attendant had spoken of were on the road to town, whizzing by at a good clip. I honked my horn at the gate until Henry came out, still chewing on his breakfast.

He waved. "So it was you. I wondered who opened the gates. Why didn't you get me up?"

I drove alongside him and waited until he swallowed. "Henry, did you hear me go out last night?"

"Me? Naw, I slept like a log. Ever since the kid was gone I couldn't sleep thinking that it was all my fault because I sleep so sound, but last night I felt pretty good."

"You must have. Two cars went out, the first one was your boss."

"York? Where'd he go?"

"To town."

He shifted uneasily from one foot to the other. "Do . . . do you think he'll be sore because I didn't hear him?"

I shook my head. "I don't think so. In fact, I don't think he wanted to be heard."

"When's he coming back?"

"He won't. He's dead." I left him standing there with his mouth open. The next time he'd be more careful of those gates.

I raced the engine outside the house and cut it. If that didn't wake everyone in the house the way I slammed the door did. Upstairs I heard a few indignant voices sounding off behind closed doors. I ran up the stairs and met Roxy at the top, holding a quilted robe together at her middle.

She shushed me with her hand. "Be quiet,

please. The boy is still asleep." It was going to be hard on him when he woke up.

"Just get up, Roxy?"

"A moment ago when you made all the noise out front. What are you doing up?"

"Never mind. Everybody still around?"

"How should I know? Why, what's the matter?"

"York's been murdered."

Her hand flew to her mouth. For a long second her breath caught in her throat. "W . . . who did it?" she stammered.

"That's what I'd like to know, Roxy."

She bit her lip. "It . . . it was like we were talking about, wasn't it?"

"Seems to be. The finger's on Myra Grange, now. It happened in her apartment and she took a powder."

"Well, what will we do?"

"You get the gang up. Don't tell them anything, just that I want to see them down in the living room. Go ahead."

Roxy was glad to be doing something. She half ran to the far end of the hall and threw herself into the first room. I walked around to Ruston's door and tried it. Locked. Roxy's door was open and I went in that way, closing it behind me, then stepped softly to the door of the adjoining room and went in.

Ruston was fast asleep, a slight smile on his face as he played in his dreams. The covers were pulled up under his chin making him look younger than his fourteen years. I blew a wisp of hair away that had drifted across his brow and shook him lightly. "Ruston."

I rocked him again. "Ruston."

His eyes came open slowly. When he saw me he smiled. "Hello, Mr. Hammer."

"Call me Mike, kid, we're pals, aren't we?"

"You bet . . . Mike." He freed one arm and stretched. "Is it time to get up?"

"No, Ruston, not yet. There's something I have to tell you." I wondered how to put it. It wasn't easy to tell a kid that the father he loved had just been butchered by a blood-crazy killer.

"What is it? You look awfully worried, Mike, is something wrong?"

"Something is very wrong, kid, are you pretty tough?"

Another shy smile. "I'm not tough, not really. I wish I were, like people in stories."

I decided to give it to him the hard way and get it over with. "Your dad's dead, son."

He didn't grasp the meaning of it at first. He looked at me, puzzled, as though he had misinterpreted what I had said.

"Dead?"

I nodded. Realization came like a flood. The tears started in the corners. One rolled down his cheek. "No . . . he can't be dead. He can't be!" I put my arms around him for a second time. He hung on to me and sobbed.

"Oh . . . Dad. What happened to him, Mike? What happened?"

Softly, I stroked his head, trying to remember

85

what my own father did with me when I hurt myself. I couldn't give him the details. "He's . . . just dead, Ruston."

"Something happened, I know." He tried to fight the tears, but it was no use. He drew away and rubbed his eyes. "What happened, Mike, please tell me?"

I handed him my handkerchief. He'd find out later, and it was better he heard it from me than one of the ghouls. "Someone killed him. Here, blow your nose." He blew, never taking his eyes from mine. I've seen puppies look at me that way when they've been kicked and didn't understand why.

"Killed? No . . . nobody would kill Dad . . . not my dad." I didn't say a word after that. I let it sink in and watched his face contort with the pain of the thought until I began to hurt in the chest myself.

For maybe ten minutes we sat like that, quietly, before the kid dried his eyes. He seemed older now. A thing like that will age anyone. His hand went to my arm. I patted his shoulder.

"Mike?"

"Yes, Ruston?"

"Do you think you can find the one who did it?"

"I'm going to try, kid."

His lips tightened fiercely. "I want you to. I wish I were big enough to. I'd shoot him, that's what I'd do!" He broke into tears again after that outburst. "Oh . . . Mike."

"You lay there, kid. Get a little rest, then when you feel better get dressed and come downstairs and we'll have a little talk. Think of something, only don't think of . . . that. It takes time to get over these things, but you will. Right now it hurts worse than anything in the world, but time will fix it up. You're tough, Ruston. After last night I'd say that you were the toughest kid that ever lived. Be tough now and don't cry anymore. Okay?"

"I'll try, Mike, honest, I'll try."

He rolled over in the bed and buried his face in the pillow. I unlocked his door to the hall and went out. I had to stick around now whether I wanted to or not. I promised the kid. And it was a promise I meant to keep.

Once before I made a promise, and I kept it. It killed my soul, but I kept it. I thought of all the blood that had run in the war, all that I had seen and had dripped on me, but none was redder or more repulsive than that blood I had seen when I kept my last promise.

Chapter Five

Their faces were those that stare at you from the walls of a museum; severe, hostile, expectant. They stood in various attitudes waiting to see what apology I had to offer for dragging them from their beds at this early hour.

Arthur Graham awkwardly sipped a glass of orange juice between swollen lips. His brother puffed nervously at a cigarette. The Ghents sat as one family in the far corner, Martha trying to be aloof as was Junior. Rhoda and her father felt conspicuous in their hurried dressing and fidgeted on the edge of their chairs.

Alice Nichols was . . . Alice. When I came into the living room she threw an eyeful of passion at me and said under her breath, "Lo, lover." It was too early for that stuff. I let the bags under my eyes tell her so. Roxy, sporting a worried frown, stopped me to say that there would be coffee ready in a few minutes. Good. They were going to need it.

I threw the ball from the scrimmage line before the opposition could break through with any bright remarks. "Rudolph York is dead. Somebody parted his hair with a cleaver up in Miss Grange's apartment."

I waited.

Martha gasped. Her husband's eyes nearly popped out, Junior and Rhoda looked at each other. Arthur choked on his orange juice and William dropped his cigarette. Behind me Alice said, "Tsk, tsk."

The silence was like an explosion, but before the echo died away Martha Ghent recovered enough to say coldly, "And where was Miss Grange?"

I shrugged. "Your guess is as good as mine." I laid it on the table then. "It's quite possible that she had nothing to do with it. Could be that someone here did the slaughtering. Before long the police are going to pay us a little visit. It's kind of late to start fixing up an alibi, but if you haven't any, you'd better think of one, fast."

While they swallowed that I turned on my heel and went out to the kitchen. Roxy had the coffee on a tray and I lifted a cup and carried it into Billy's room. He woke up as soon as I turned the knob.

"Hi, Mike." He looked at the clock. "What're you doing up?"

"I haven't been to bed yet. York's dead."

"What!"

"Last night. Got it with a cleaver."

"Good night! What happens now?"

"The usual routine for a while, I guess. Listen, were you in the sack all this time?"

"Hell, yes. Wait a minute, Mike, you . . ."

"Can you prove it? I mean did anyone see you there?"

"No. I've been alone. You don't think . . ."

"Quit worrying, Billy. Dilwick will be on this case and he's liable to have it in for you. That skunk will get back at you if he can't at me. He's got what little law there is in this town on his side now. What I want to do is establish some way you can prove you were here. Think of any?"

He put his finger to his mouth. "Yeah, I might at that. Twice last night I thought I heard a car go out."

"That'd be York then me."

"Right after the first car, someone came downstairs. I heard 'em inside, then there was some funny sound like somebody coughing real softly, then it died out. I couldn't figure out what it was."

"That might do it if we can find out who came down. Just forget all about it until you're asked, understand?"

"Sure, Mike. Geez, why did this have to happen? I'll be out on my ear now." His head dropped into his hands. "What'll I do?"

"We'll think of something. If you feel okay you'd better get dressed. York's car is still downtown, and when the cops get done with it you'll have to drive it back."

I handed him the coffee and he drank it gratefully. When he finished I took it away and went into the kitchen. Harvey was there drying his eyes on a handkerchief. He saw me and sniffed, "It's terrible, sir. Miss Malcom just told me. Who could have done such a thing?"

"I don't know, Harvey. Whoever it was will pay for it. Look, I'm going to climb into bed. When the police come, get me up, will you?"

"Of course, sir. Will you eat first?"

"No thanks, later."

I skirted the living room and pushed myself up the stairs. The old legs were tired out. The bedclothes were where I had thrown them, in a heap at the foot of the bed. I didn't even bother to take off my shoes. When I put my head down I didn't care if the house burned to the ground as long as nobody awakened me.

The police came and went. Their voices came to me through the veil of sleep, only partially coherent. Voices of insistence, voices of protest and indignation. A woman's voice raised in anger and a meeker man's voice supporting it. Nobody seemed to care whether I was there or not, so I let the veil swirl into a gray shroud that shut off all sounds and thoughts.

It was the music that woke me. A terrible storm of music that reverberated through the house like a hurricane, shrieking in a wonderful agony. There had never been music like that before. I listened to the composition, wondering. For a space of seconds it was a song of rage, then it dwindled to a dirge of sorrow. No bar or theme was repeated.

I slipped out of the bed and opened the door, letting the full force of it hit me. It was impossible to conceive that a piano could tell such a story as this one was telling.

He sat there at the keyboard, a pitiful little figure clad in a Prussian blue bathrobe. His head was thrown back, the eyes shut tightly as if in pain, his fingers beating notes of anguish from the keys.

He was torturing himself with it. I sat beside him. "Ruston, don't."

Abruptly, he ceased in the middle of the concert and let his head fall to his chest. The critics were right when they acclaimed him a genius. If only they could have heard his latest recital.

"You have to take it easy, kid. Remember what I told you."

"I know, Mike, I'll try to be better. I just keep thinking of Dad all the time."

"He meant a lot to you, didn't he?"

"Everything. He taught me so many things, music, art . . . things that it takes people so long to get to know. He was wonderful, the best dad ever."

Without speaking I walked him over to the big chair beside the fireplace and sat down on the arm of the chair beside him. "Ruston," I started, "your father isn't here anymore, but he wouldn't want you to grieve about it. I think he'd rather you went on with all those things he was teaching you, and be what he wanted you to be."

"I will be, Mike," he said. His voice lacked color, but it rang earnestly. "Dad wanted me to excel in everything. He often told me that a man never lived long enough to accomplish nearly anything he was capable of because it took too long to learn the fundamentals. That's why he wanted me to know all these things while I was young. Then when I was a doctor or a scientist maybe I would be ahead of myself, sort of."

He was better as long as he could talk. Let him get it out of his system, I thought. It's the only way. "You've done fine, kid. I bet he was proud of you."

"Oh, he was. I only wish he could have been able to make his report."

"What report?"

"To the College of Scientists. They meet every five years to turn in reports, then one is selected as being the best one and the winner is elected President of the College for a term. He wanted that awfully badly. His report was going to be on me."

"I see," I said. "Maybe Miss Grange will do it for him."

I shouldn't have said that. He looked up at me woefully. "I don't think she will, not after the police find her."

It hit me right between the eyes. "Who's been telling you things, kid?"

"The policemen were here this morning. The big one made us all tell where we were last night and everything. Then he told us about Miss Grange."

"What about her?"

"They found her car down by the creek. They think she drowned herself."

I could have tossed a brick through a window right then. "Harvey!" I yelled. "Hey, Harvey."

93

The butler came in on the double. "I thought I asked you to wake me up when the police got here. What the hell happened?"

"Yes, sir. I meant to, but Officer Dilwick suggested that I let you sleep. I'm sorry, sir, it was more an order than a request."

So that was how things stood. I'd get even with that fat slob. "Where is everybody?"

"After the police took their statements he directed the family to return to their own homes. Miss Malcom and Parks are bringing Mr. York's car home. Sergeant Price wished me to tell you that he will be at the headquarters on the highway this evening and he would like to see you."

"I'm glad someone would like to see me," I remarked. I turned to Ruston. "I'm going to leave, son. How about you going to your room until Roxy . . . I mean Miss Malcom gets here? Okay?"

"All right, Mike. Why did you call her Roxy?"

"I have pet names for everybody."

"Do you have one for me?" he asked, little lights dancing in his eyes.

"You bet."

"What?"

"Sir Lancelot. He was the bravest of the brave."

As I walked out of the room I heard him repeat it softly. "Sir Lancelot, the bravest of the brave."

I reached the low fieldstone building set back from the road at a little after eight. The sky was threatening again, the air chilly and humid. Little beads of sweat were running down the windshield on the side. A sign across the drive read, STATE

94

POLICE HEADQUARTERS, and I parked beside it.

Sergeant Price was waiting for me. He nodded when I came in and lay down the sheaf of papers he was examining. I threw my hat on an empty desk and helped myself to a chair. "Harvey gave me your message," I said. "What's the story?"

He leaned back in the swivel seat and tapped the desk with a pen. "We found Grange's car."

"So I heard. Find her yet?"

"No. The door was open and her body may have washed out. If it did we won't find it so easily. The tide was running out and would have taken the body with it. The river runs directly into the bay, you know."

"That's all supposition. She may not have been in the car."

He put the pencil between his teeth. "Every indication points to the fact that she was. There are clear tire marks showing where the car was deliberately wrenched off the road before the guardrails to the bridge. The car was going fast, besides. It landed thirty feet out in the water."

"That's not what you wanted to see me about?" I put in.

"You're on the ball, Mr. Hammer."

"Mike. I hate titles."

"Okay, Mike. What I want is this kidnapping deal."

"Figuring a connection?"

"There may be one if Grange was murdered."

I grinned. "You're on the ball yourself." Once

again I went over the whole story, starting with Billy's call when he was arrested. He listened intently without saying a word until I was finished.

"What do you think?" he asked.

"Somebody's going to a lot of trouble."

"Do you smell a correlation between the two?"

I squinted at him. "I don't know . . . yet. That kidnapping came at the wrong time. A kidnapper wants money. This one never got away with his victim. Generally speaking, it isn't likely that a second try would be made on the same person, but York wanted the whole affair hushed up ostensibly for fear of the publicity it would bring. That would leave the kid open again. It is possible that the kidnapper, enraged at having his deal busted open, would hang around waiting to get even with York and saw his chance when he took off at that hour of the morning to see Grange."

Price shook out a cig from his pack and offered me one. "If that was the case, money would not have been the primary motive. A kidnapper who has muffed his snatch wants to get far away fast."

I lit up and blew a cloud of smoke at the ceiling. "Sounds screwed up, doesn't it?" He agreed. "Did you find out that York didn't have long to live anyway?"

He seemed startled at the change of subject. "No. Why?"

"Let's do it this way," I said. "York was on the list. He had only a few years at best to live. At the bottom of every crime there's a motive no matter how remote, and nine times out of ten that motive is cold, hard cash. He's got a bunch of relations that have been hanging around waiting for him to kick the bucket for a long time. One of them might have known that his condition was so bad that any excitement might knock him off. That one arranges a kidnapping, then when it fails takes direct action by knocking off York, making it look like Grange did it, then kills Grange to further the case by making it appear that she was a suicide in a fit of remorse."

Price smiled gently. "Are you testing me? I could shoot holes in that with a popgun. Arranging for a kidnapping means that you invite blackmail and lose everything you tried to get. York comes into it somewhere along the line because he was searching for something in that apartment. Try me again."

I laughed. "No good. You got all the answers."

He shoved the papers across the desk to me. "There are the statements of everybody in the house. They seem to support each other pretty well. Nobody left the house according to them so nobody had a chance to knock off York. That puts it outside the house again."

I looked them over. Not much there. Each sheet was an individual statement and it barely covered a quarter of the page. Besides a brief personal history was the report that once in bed, each person had remained there until I called them into the living room that morning.

I handed them back. "Somebody's lying. Is this all you got?"

"We didn't press for information although

Dilwick wanted to. Who lied?"

"Somebody. Billy Parks told me he heard someone come downstairs during the night."

"Could it have been you?"

"No, it was before I followed York."

"He made no mention of it to me."

"Probably because he's afraid somebody will refute it if he does just to blacken him. I half promised him I'd check on it first."

"I see. Did York take you into his confidence at any time?"

"Nope. I didn't know him that long. After the snatch he hired me to stick around until he was certain his son was safe."

Price threw the pencil on the desk. "We're climbing a tree," he said tersely. "York was killed for a reason. Myra Grange was killed for the same reason. I think that for the time being we'll concentrate our efforts on locating Grange's body. When we're sure of her death we can have something definite to work on. Meanwhile I'm taking it for granted that she is dead."

I stood up to leave. "I'm not taking anything for granted, Sergeant. If she's dead she's out of it; if not the finger is still on her. I'm going to play around a little bit and see what happens. What's Dilwick doing?"

"Like you. He won't believe she's dead until he sees her either."

"Don't underestimate that hulk," I told him. "He's had a lot of police work and he's shrewd. Too shrewd, in fact, that's why he was booted off the New York force. He'll be looking out for himself when the time comes. If anything develops I'll let you know."

"Do that. See you later."

That ended the visit. I went out to the car and sat behind the wheel a while, thinking. Kidnapping, murder, a disappearance. A house full of black sheep. One nice kid, an ex-stripper for a nurse and a chauffeur with a record. The butler, maybe the butler did it. Someday a butler would do it for a change. A distraught father who stuck his hand in a hole in the fireplace and found something gone. He sets out to kill and gets killed instead. The one he wanted to kill is gone, perhaps dead too. Mallory. That was the name that started the ball of murder rolling. But Mallory figured in the kidnapping.

Okay, first things first. The kidnapping was first and I'd take it that way. It was a hell of a mess. The only thing that could make it any worse was to have Grange show up with an airtight alibi. I hated to hold out on Price about Mallory, but if he had it Dilwick would have to get it too, and that would put the kibosh on me. Like hell. I promised the kid.

I shoved the car in gear and spun out on the highway. Initial clue, the cops call it, the hand that puts the hound on the trail, that's what I had to have. York thought it was in Grange's apartment. Find what he was searching for and you had the answer. Swell, let's find it.

This time I parked around the block. The rain

had started again, a light mist that you breathed into your lungs and dampened matches in your pocket. From the back of the car I pulled a slicker and climbed into it, turning the collar up high. I walked back to Main Street, crossed over to the side of the street opposite the apartment and joined the few late workers in their dash toward home.

I saw what I was looking for, a black, unmarked sedan occupied by a pair of cigar-smoking gentlemen who were trying their best to remain unnoticed. They did a lousy job. I circled the block until I was behind the apartment. A row of modest one-family houses faced me, their windows lighted with gaiety and cheer. Each house was flanked by a driveway.

Without waiting I picked the right one and turned down the cinder drive, staying to the side in the shadow of a hedgerow where the grass partially muffled my feet. Somehow I slipped between the garage and the hedges to the back fence without making too much of a racket. For ten minutes I stood that way, motionless. It wasn't a new experience for me. I remembered other pits of blackness where little brown men waited and threw jeers into our faces to draw us out. That was a real test of patience. This guy was easier. When another ten minutes passed the match lit his face briefly, then subsided into the ill-concealed glow of a cigarette tip.

Dilwick wasn't taking any chances on Myra Grange slipping back to her apartment. Or anyone else for that matter.

100

Once I had him spotted I kept my eyes a few feet to the side of him so I wouldn't lose him. Look directly at an object in the dark and you draw a blank spot. I went over the fence easily enough, then flanked the lookout by staying in the shadows again. By the time I reached the apartment building I had him silhouetted against the lights of another house. The janitor had very conveniently left a row of ash barrels stacked by the cellar entrance. I got up that close, at least. Six feet away on the other side of the gaping cavern of the entrance the law stood on flat feet, breathing heavily, cursing the rain under his breath.

My fingers snaked over the lip of a barrel, came away with a piece of ash the size of a marble. I balanced it on my thumb, then flipped it. I heard nothing, but he heard it and turned his head, that was all. I tried again with the same results. The next time I used a bigger piece. I got better results, too. He dropped the butt, ground it under his heel and walked away from the spot.

As soon as he moved I ducked around the barrels and down the stairs, then waited again, flattened against the wall. Finding nothing, the cop resumed his post. I went on tiptoes down the corridor, my hand out in front like a sleepwalker.

This part was going to take clever thinking. If they had both exits covered it was a sure bet that the apartment door was covered, too. I came to a bend in the tunnel and found myself in the furnace room. Overhead a dim bulb struggled against dust and cobwebs to send out a feeble glow. On the other side of the room a flight of metal steps led to the floor above. Sweet, but not practical. If I could make the roof I might be able to come down the fire escape, but that meant a racket or being seen by the occupants.

Right then I was grateful to the inventor of the dumbwaiter. The empty box yawned at me with a sleepy invitation. The smell was bad, but it was worth it. I climbed aboard and gave the rope a tentative pull to see if the pulleys squealed. They were well oiled. *Danke schön,* janitor. You get an *A*.

When I passed the first floor I was beginning to doubt whether I could make it all the way. Crouching there like that I had no leverage to bear on the ropes. It was all wrist motion. I took a hitch in the rope around the catch on the sliding door and rested a second, then began hauling away again. Somewhere above me voices passed back and forth. Someone yelled, 'Put it on the dumbwaiter.'

I held my breath. Let them catch me here and I was sunk. Dilwick would like nothing better than to get me on attempted burglary and work me over with a few of his boys.

A moment went by, two, then, "Later, honey, it's only half-full."

Thanks, pal. Remind me to scratch your back. I got another grip on the rope and pulled away. By the time I reached Myra's door I was exhausted. Fortunately, one of the cops had forgotten to lock it after taking a peek down the well, not that it mattered. I didn't care whether anyone was inside or not. I shoved the two-bit door open and tumbled to the floor. I was lucky. The house was quiet as a tomb. If I ever see that trick pulled in a movie and the hero steps out looking fresh as a daisy I'll throw rocks at the screen. I lay there until I got my wind back.

The flash I used had the lens taped, so the only light it shed was a round disk the size of a quarter. I poked around the kitchen a bit taking it all in. Nobody had cleaned up since the murder as far as I could see. I went into the living room, avoiding the litter on the floor. The place was even worse than it was before. The police had finished what York had started, pulling drawers open further, tearing the pictures from the walls and scuffing up the rug.

But they hadn't found it. If they had I wouldn't've had to use the dumbwaiter to get in. Dilwick was better than shrewd. He was waiting for Grange to come back and find it for him.

Which meant that he was pretty certain Grange was alive. Dilwick knew something that Price and I didn't know, in that case.

In the first half hour I went through every piece of junk that had been dragged out without coming across anything worthwhile. I kicked at the pile and tried the drawers in the desk again. My luck stunk; Grange didn't go in for false bottoms or double walls. I thought of every place a dame hides things, but the cops had thought of them too. Every corner had been poked into, every closet emptied out. Women think of cute places like the hollows of bedposts and the inside of lamps, but the bedposts turned out to be solid and the lamps of modern transparent glass.

Hell, she had to have important things around. College degrees, insurance policies and that sort of stuff. I finally realized what was wrong. My psychology. Or hers. She only resembled a woman. She looked like one and dressed like one, physically, she was one, but Myra Grange had one of those twisted complexes. If she thought it was like a man. That was better. Being partially a woman she would want to secrete things; being part man she would hide them in a place not easily accessible, where it would take force, and not deduction to locate the cache.

I started grinning then. I pulled the cabinets away from the walls and tried the sills of the doors. When I found a hollow behind the radiator I felt better. It was dust-filled and hadn't been used for some time, mainly because a hand reaching in there could be burned if the heat was on, but I knew I was on the right track.

It took time, but I found it when I was on my hands and knees, shooting light along the baseboards under the bed. It wasn't even a good job of concealment. I saw where a claw hammer had probably knocked a hole in the plaster behind it.

A package of envelopes held together by a large rubber band was the treasure. It was four-inches thick, at least, with corners of stock certificates showing in the middle. A nice little pile.

I didn't waste time going through them then. I stuck the package inside my coat and buttoned the slicker over it. I had one end of the baseboard in place when I thought what a fine joke it would be to pull on slobbermouth to leave a calling card. With a wrench I pulled it loose, laid it on the floor where it couldn't be missed and got out to the kitchen. Let my fat friend figure that one out. He'd have the jokers at the doors shaking in their shoes by the time he was done with them.

The trip down was better. All I had to do was hang on and let the rope slide through my hands. Between the first floor and the basement I tightened up on the hemp and cut down the descent. It was a good landing, just a slight jar and I walked away from there. Getting out was easier than coming in. I poked my head out the cellar window on the side where the walk led around to the back and the concrete stared me in the face, gave a short whistle and called, "Hey, Mac."

It was enough. Heavy feet came pounding around the side and I made a dash up the corridor, out the door and dived into the bushes before the puzzled cop got back to his post scratching his head in bewilderment. The fence, the driveway, and I was in my car pulling up the street behind a trailer truck.

The package was burning a hole in my pocket. I turned down a side street where the neon of an open diner provided a stopping-off place, parked and went in and occupied a corner booth. When a skinny waiter in an oversized apron took my order I extracted the bundle. I rifled through the deck, ignoring the bonds and policies. I found what I was after.

It was York's will, made out two years ago, leaving every cent of his dough to Grange. If that female was still alive this put her on the spot for sure. Here was motive, pure, raw motive. A several-million-dollar motive, but it might as well be a can tied to her tail. She was a lucky one indeed if she lived to enjoy it.

Sloppy Joe came back with my hamburgers and coffee. I shelved the package while he dished out the slop, then forced it down my gullet, with the coffee as a lubricant. I was nearly through when I noticed my hands. They were dusty as hell. I noticed something else, too. The rubber band that had been around the package lay beside my coffee cup, stiff and rotted, and in two pieces.

Then I didn't get it after all, at least not what York was searching for. This package hadn't been opened for a hell of a long time, and it was a good bet that whatever had been in the fireplace had been there until the other night. The will had been placed in the package years ago.

Damn. Say it again, Mike, you outsmarted yourself that time. Damn.

Chapter Six

I set my watch by the clock on the corner while I waited for the light to change. Nine-fifteen, and all was far from well. Just what the hell was it that threw York into a spasm? I knew damn well now that whatever it was, either Grange had it with her or she never had it at all. I was right back where I started from. Which left two things to be done. Find Mallory, or see who came downstairs the night of the murder and why that movement was denied in the statements. All right, let it be Mallory. Maybe Roxy could supply some answers. I pulled the will from the package and slipped it inside my jacket, then tossed the rest of the things in the back of the glove compartment.

Henry had the gates open as soon as I turned off the road. When he shut them behind me I called him over. "Anyone been here while I was gone?"

"Yes, sir. The undertaker came, but that was all."

I thanked him and drove up the drive. Harvey nodded solemnly when he opened the door and took my hat. "Have there been any developments, sir?"

"Not a thing. Where's Miss Malcom?"

"Upstairs, I believe. She took Master Ruston to his room a little while ago. Shall I call her for you?"

"Never mind, I'll go up myself."

I rapped lightly and opened the door at the same time. Roxy took a quick breath, grabbed the negligee off the bed and held it in front of her. That split second of visioning nudity that was classic beauty made the blood pound in my ears. I shut my eyes against it. "Easy, Roxy," I said, "I can't see so don't scream and don't throw things. I didn't mean it."

She laughed lightly. "Oh, for heaven's sake, open them up. You've seen me like this before." I looked just as she tied the wrapper around her. That kind of stuff could drive a guy bats.

"Don't tempt me. I thought you'd changed?"

"Mike . . . don't say it that way. Maybe I have gone modest, but I like it better. In your rough way you respected it too, but I can't very well heave things at you for seeing again what you saw so many times before."

"The kid asleep?"

"I think so." The door was open a few inches, the other room dark. I closed it softly, then went back and sat on the edge of the bed. Roxy dragged the chair from in front of her vanity and set it down before me.

"Do I get sworn in first?" she asked with a fake pout.

"This is serious."

"Shoot."

108

"I'm going to mention a name to you. Don't answer me right away. Let it sink in, think about it, think of any time since you've been here that you might have heard it, no matter when. Roll it around on your tongue a few times until it becomes familiar, then if you recognize it tell me where or when you heard it and who said it . . . if you can."

"I see. Who is it?"

I handed her a cigarette and plucked one myself. "Mallory," I said as I lit it for her. I hooked my hands around my knee and waited. Roxy blew smoke at the floor. She looked up at me a couple of times, her eyes vacant with thought, mouthing the name to herself. I watched her chew on her lip and suck in a lungful of smoke.

Finally she rubbed her hand across her forehead and grimaced. "I can't remember ever having heard it," she told me. "Is it very important?"

"I think it might be. I don't know."

"I'm sorry, Mike." She leaned forward and patted my knee.

"Hell, don't take it to heart. He's just a name to me. Do you think any of the characters might know anything?"

"That I couldn't say. York was a quiet one, you know."

"I didn't know. Did he seem to favor any of them?"

She stood up and stretched on her toes. Under the sheer fabric little muscles played in her body. "As far as I could see, he had an evident distaste for the lot of them. When I first came here he apparently liked his niece, Rhoda. He remembered her with gifts upon the slightest provocation. Expensive ones, too. I know, I bought them for him."

I snubbed my butt. "Uh-huh. Did he turn to someone else?"

"Why, yes." She looked at me in faint surprise. "The other niece, Alice Nichols."

"I would have looked at her first to begin with."

"Yes, you would," she grinned. "Shall I go on?"

"Please."

"For quite a while she got all the attention which threw the Ghents into an uproar. I imagine they saw Rhoda being his heir and didn't like the switch. Mr. York's partiality to Alice continued for several months then fell off somewhat. He paid little attention to her after that, but never forgot her on birthdays or holidays. His gifts were as great as ever. And that," she concluded, "is the only unusual situation that ever existed as far as I know."

"Alice and York, huh? How far did the relationship go?"

"Not that far. His feelings were paternal, I think."

"Are you sure?"

"Pretty sure. Mr. York was long past his prime. If sex meant anything to him it was no more than a biological difference between the species."

"It might mean something to Alice."

"Of that I'm sure. She likes anything with muscles, but with Mr. York she didn't need it. She

110

did all right without it. I noticed that she cast a hook in your direction."

"She didn't use the right bait," I stated briefly. "She showed up in my room with nothing on but a prayer and wanted to play. I like to be teased a little. Besides, I was tired. Did York know she acted that way?"

Roxy plugged in a tiny radio set and fiddled with the dial. "If he did he didn't care."

"Kitten, did York ever mention a will?"

An old Benny Goodman tune came on. She brought it in clearer and turned around with a dance step. "Yes, he had one. He kept the family on the verge of a nervous breakdown every time he alluded to it, but he never came right out and said where his money would go."

She began to spin with the music. "Hold still a second will you. Didn't he hand out any hints at all?"

The hem of her negligee brushed past my face, higher than any hem had a right to be. "None at all, except that it would go where it was most deserving."

Her legs flashed in the light. My heart began beating faster again. They were lovely legs, long, firm. "Did Grange ever hear that statement?"

She stopped, poised dramatically and threw her belt at me. "Yes." She began to dance again. The music was a rhumba now and her body swayed to it, jerking rhythmically. "Once during a heated discussion Mr. York told them all that Miss Grange was the only one he could trust and she would

111

be the one to handle his estate."

There was no answer to that. How the devil could she handle it if she got it all? I never got a chance to think about it. The robe came off and she used it like a fan, almost disclosing everything, showing nothing. Her skin was fair, cream-colored, her body graceful. She circled in front of me, letting her hair fall to her shoulders. At the height of that furious dance I stood up.

Roxy flew into my arms. "Kiss me . . . you thing."

I didn't need any urging.

Her mouth melted into mine like butter. I felt her nails digging into my arms. Roughly, I pushed her away, held her there at arm's length. "What was that for?"

She gave me a delightfully evil grin. "That is because I could love you if I wanted to, Mike. I did once, you know."

"I know. What made you stop?"

"You're Broadway, Mike. You're the bright lights and big money . . . sometimes. You're bullets when there should be kisses. That's why I stopped. I wanted someone with a normal life expectancy."

"Then why this?"

"I missed you. Funny as it sounds, someplace inside me I have a spot that's always reserved for you. I didn't want you to ever know it, but there it is."

I kissed her again, longer and closer this time. Her body was talking to me, screaming to me.

There would have been more if Ruston hadn't called out.

Roxy slipped into the robe again, the cold static making it snap. "Let me go," I said. She nodded.

I opened the door and hit the light switch. "Hello, Sir Lancelot." The kid had been crying in his sleep, but he smiled at me.

"Hello, Mike. When did you come?"

"A little while ago. Want something?"

"Can I have some water, please? My throat's awfully dry."

A pitcher half-full of ice was on the desk. I poured it into a glass, and handed it to him and he drank deeply. "Have enough?"

He gave the glass back to me. "Yes, thank you."

I gave his chin a little twist. "Then back to bed with you. Get a good sleep."

Ruston squirmed back under the covers. "I will. Good night, Mike."

"'Night, pal." I closed the door behind me. Roxy had changed into a deep maroon quilted job and sat in the chair smoking a cigarette. The moment had passed. I could see that she was sorry, too. She handed me my deck of butts and I pocketed them, then waved a good-night. Neither of us felt like saying anything.

Evidently Harvey had retired for the night. The staircase was lit only by tiny night-lights shaped to resemble candle flames, while the foyer below was a dim challenge to the eyesight. I picked my way through the rooms and found Billy's without upsetting anything. He was in bed, but awake.

"It's Mike, Billy," I said.

He snapped on the bed lamp. "Come on in."

I shut the door and slumped in a chair next to him. "More questions. I know it's late, but I hope you don't mind."

"Not at all, Mike. What's new?"

"Oh, you know how these things are. Haven't found Miss Grange yet and things are settling around her. Dilwick's got his men covering her place like a blanket."

"Yeah? What for? Ain't she supposed to be drowned?"

"Somebody wants it to look that way, I think. Listen, Billy, you told me before that you heard someone come downstairs between York and me the night of the murder. It wasn't important before except to establish an alibi for you if it was needed, but now what you heard may have a bearing on the case. Go over it again, will you? Do it in as much detail as you can."

"Let's see. I didn't really hear York leave, I just remember a car crunching the gravel. It woke me up. I had a headache and a bad taste in my mouth from something York gave me. Pills, I think."

"It was supposed to keep you asleep. He gave you a sedative."

"Whatever it was I puked up in bed, that's why it didn't do me any good. Anyway, I lay here half-awake when I heard somebody come down the last two stairs. They squeak, they do. This room is set funny, see. Any noise outside the room travels right in here. They got a name for it."

"Acoustics."

"Yeah, that's it. That's why nobody ever used this room but me. They couldn't stand the noise all the time. Not only loud noises, any kind of noises. This was like whoever it was didn't want to make a sound, but it didn't do any good because I heard it. Only I thought it was one of the family trying to be quiet so they wouldn't wake anyone up and I didn't pay any attention to it. About two or three minutes after that comes this noise like someone coughing with their head under a coat and it died out real slow and that's all. I was just getting back to sleep when there was another car tearing out the drive. That was you, I guess."

"That all?"

"Yeah, that's all, Mike. I went back to sleep after that."

This was the ace. It had its face down so I couldn't tell whether it was red or black, but it was the ace. The bells were going off in my head again, those little tinkles that promised to become the pealing of chimes. The cart was before the horse, but if I could find the right buckle to unloosen I could put them right back.

"Billy, say nothing to nobody about this, understand? If the local police question you, say nothing. If Sergeant Price wants to know things, have him see me. If you value your head, keep your mouth shut and your door locked."

His eyes popped wide open. "Geez, Mike, is it that important?"

I nodded. "I have a funny feeling, Billy, that the noises you heard were made by the murderer."

"Good Golly!" It left him breathless. Then, "You . . . you think the killer . . ." he swallowed, ". . . might make a try for me?"

"No, Billy, not the killer. You aren't that important to him. Someone else might, though. I think we have a lot more on our hands than just plain murder."

"What?" It was a hoarse whisper.

"Kidnapping, for one thing. That comes in somewhere. You sit tight until you hear from me." Before I left I turned with my hand on the knob and looked into his scared face again. "Who's Mallory, Billy?"

"Mallory who?"

"Just Mallory."

"Gosh, I don't know."

"Okay, kid, thanks."

Mallory. He might as well be Smith or Jones. So far he was just a word. I navigated the gloom again half consciously, thinking of him. Mallory of the kidnapping; Mallory whose very name turned York white and added a link to the chain of crime. Somewhere Mallory was sitting on his fanny getting a large charge out of the whole filthy mess. York knew who he was, but York was dead. Could that be the reason for his murder? Likely. York, by indirect implication and his peculiar action intimated that Myra Grange knew of him too, but she was dead or missing. Was that Mallory's doing? Likely. Hell, I couldn't put my

116

finger on anything more definite than a vague possibility. Something had to blow up, somebody would have to try to take the corners out of one of the angles. I gathered all the facts together, but they didn't make sense. A name spoken, the speaker unseen; someone who came downstairs at night, unseen too, and denying it; a search for a stolen something-or-other, whose theft was laid at the feet of the vanished woman. I muttered a string of curses under my breath and kicked aimlessly at empty air. Where was there to start? Dilwick would have his feelers out for Grange and so would Price. With that many men they could get around much too fast for me. Besides, I had the feeling that she was only part of it all, not the key figure that would unlock the mystery, but more like one whose testimony would cut down a lot of time and work. I still couldn't see her putting the cleaver into York then doing the Dutch afterward. If she was associated with him professionally she would have to be brilliant, and great minds either turn at murder or attempt to conceive of a flawless plot. York's death was brutal. It was something you might find committed in a dark alley in a slum section for a few paltry dollars, or in a hotel room when a husband returns to find his woman in the arms of her lover. A passion kill, a revenge kill, a crude murder for small money, yes, but did any of these motives fit here? For whom did York hold passion . . . or vice versa? Roxy hit it when she said he was too old. Small money? None was gone from his wallet apparently.

117

That kind of kill would take place outside on a lonely road or on a deserted street anyway. Revenge . . . revenge. Grange said he had no enemies. That was now. Could anything have happened in the past? You could almost rule that out too, on the basis of precedent. Revenge murders usually happen soon after the event that caused the desire for revenge. If the would-be murderer has time to think he realizes the penalty for murder and it doesn't happen. Unless, of course, the victim, realizing what might happen, keeps on the move. That accentuates the importance of the event to the killer and spurs him on. Negative. York was a public figure for years. He had lived in the same house almost twenty years. Big money, a motive for anything. Was that it, Grange came into that. Why did she have the will? Those things are kept in a safe deposit box or lawyer's files. The chief beneficiary rarely ever got to see the document much less have it hidden among her personal effects for so long a time. Damn, Grange had told me she had a large income aside from what York gave her. She didn't care what he did with his money. What a very pretty attitude to take, especially when you know where it's going. She could afford to be snotty with me. I remembered her face when she said it, aloof, the hell-with-it attitude. Why the act if it wasn't important then? What was she trying to put across?

Myra Grange. I didn't want it to, but it came back to her every time. Missing the night of the kidnapping; seen on the road, but she said no. Why? I started to grin a little. An unmarried per-

118

son goes out at night for what reason? Natch . . . a date. Grange had a date, and her kind of dates had to be kept behind closed doors, that's why she was rarely seen about. York wouldn't want it to get around either for fear of criticism, that's why he was nice about it. Grange would deny it for a lot of reasons. It would hurt her professionally, or worse, she might lose a perfectly good girl friend. It was all supposition, but I bet I was close.

The night air hit me in the face. I hadn't realized I was standing outside the door until a chilly mist ran up the steps and bugged me. I stuck my hands in my pockets and walked down the drive. Behind me the house watched with staring eyes. I wished it could talk. The gravel path encircled the gloomy old place with gray arms and I followed it aimlessly, trying to straighten out my thoughts. When I came to the fork I stood motionless a moment then followed the turn off to the right.

Fifty yards later the colorless bulk of the laboratory grew out of the darkness like a crypt. It was a drab cinder-block building, the only incongruous thing on the estate. No windows broke the contours of the walls on either of the two sides visible, no place where prying eyes might observe what occurred within. At the far end a thirty-foot chimney poked a skinny finger skyward, stretching to clear the tree-tops. Upon closer inspection a ventilation system showed just under the eaves, screened air intakes and outlets above eye level.

I went around the building once, a hundred-by-fifty-foot structure, but the only opening was the single steel door in the front, a door built to withstand weather or siege. But it was not built to withstand curiosity. The first master key I used turned the lock. It was a laugh. The double tongue had prongs as thick as my thumb, but the tumbler arrangement was as uncomplicated as a glass of milk.

Fortunately, the light pulls had tiny phosphorescent tips that cast a greenish glow. I reached up and yanked one. Overhead a hundred-watt bulb flared into daylight brilliance. I checked the door and shut it, then looked about me. Architecturally, the building was a study in simplicity. One long corridor ran the length of it. Off each side were rooms, perhaps sixteen in all. No dirt marred the shining marble floor, no streaks on the enameled white walls. Each door was shut, the brass of the knobs gleaming, the woodwork smiling in varnished austerity. For all its rough exterior, the inside was spotless.

The first room on the one side was an office, fitted with a desk, several filing cabinets, a big chair and a water cooler. The room opposite was its mate. So far so good. I could tell by the pipe rack which had been York's.

Next came some sort of supply room. In racks along the walls were hundreds of labeled bottles, chemicals unknown to me. I opened the bins below. Electrical fittings, tubes, meaningless coils of copper tubing lay neatly placed on shelves alongside instruments and parts of unusual design.

This time the room opposite was no mate. Crouched in one corner was a generator, snuggling up to a transformer. Wrist-thick power lines came in through the door, passed through the two units and into the walls. I had seen affairs like this on portable electric chairs in some of our more rural states. I couldn't figure this one out. If the education of Ruston was York's sole work, why all the gadgets? Or was that merely a shield for something bigger?

The following room turned everything into a cockeyed mess. Here was a lounge that was sheer luxury. Overstuffed chairs, a seven-foot couch, a chair shaped like a French curve that went down your back, up under your knees and ended in a cushioned foot rest. Handy to everything were magazine racks of popular titles and some of more obscure titles. Books in foreign languages rested between costly jade bookends. A combination radio-phonograph sat in the corner, flanked by cabinets of symphonic and pop records. Opposite it at the other end of the room was a grand piano with operatic scores concealed in the seat. Cleverly contrived furniture turned into art boards and reading tables. A miniature refrigerator housed a bottle of ice water and several frosted glasses. Along the wall several Petri dishes held agar — agar with yellow bacteria cultures mottling the tops. Next to them was a double-lensed microscope of the best manufacture.

What a playpen. Here anyone could relax in comfort with his favorite hobby. Was this where

Ruston spent his idle hours? There was nothing here for a boy, but his mind would appreciate it.

It was getting late. I shut the door and moved on, taking quick peeks into each room. A full-scale lab, test tubes, retorts, a room of books, nothing but books, then more electrical equipment. I crossed the corridor and stuck my head in. I had to take a second look to be sure I was right. If that wasn't the hot seat standing in the middle of the floor it was a good imitation.

I didn't get a chance to go over it. Very faintly I heard metal scratching against metal. I pulled the door shut and ran down the corridor, pulling at the light cords as I went. I wasn't the only one that was curious this night.

Just as I closed the door of Grange's office behind me the outside door swung inward. Someone was standing there in the dark waiting. I heard his breath coming hard with an attempt to control it. The door shut, and a sliver of light ran along the floor, shining through the crack onto my shoes. The intruder wasn't bothering with the overheads, he was using a flash.

A hand touched the knob. In two shakes I was palming my rod, holding it above my head ready to bring it down the second he stepped in the door. It never opened. He moved to the other side and went into York's office instead.

As slowly as I could I eased the knob around, then brought it toward my stomach. An inch, two, then there was room enough to squeeze out. I kept the dark paneling of the door at my back, stood there in the darkness, letting my breath in and out silently while I watched Junior Ghent rifle York's room.

He had the flashlight propped on the top of the desk, working in its beam. He didn't seem to be in a hurry. He pulled out every drawer of the files, scattering their contents on the floor in individual piles. When he finished with one row he moved to another until the empty cabinet gaped like a toothless old man.

For a second I thought he was leaving and faded to one side, but all he did was turn the flash to focus on the other side of the room. Again, he repeated the procedure. I watched.

At the end of twenty minutes his patience began to give out. He yanked things viciously from place and kicked at the chair, then obviously holding himself in check tried to be calm about it. In another fifteen minutes he had circled the room, making it look like a bomb had gone off in there. He hadn't found what he was after.

That came by accident.

The chair got in his way again. He pushed it so hard it skidded along the marble, hit an empty drawer and toppled over. I even noticed it before he did.

The chair had a false bottom.

Very clever. Search a room for hours and you'll push furniture all over the place, but how often will you turn up a chair and inspect it. Junior let out a surprised gasp and went down on his knees, his fingers running over the paneling. When his fingernails didn't work he took a screwdriver from his pocket and forced it into the wood. There was a sharp snap and the bottom was off.

A thick envelope was fastened to a wire clasp. He smacked his lips and wrenched it free. With his forefinger he lifted the flap and drew out a sheaf of papers. These he scanned quickly, let out a sarcastic snort, and discarded them on the floor. He dug into the envelope and brought out something else. He studied it closely, rubbing his hand over his stomach. Twice he adjusted his glasses and held them closer to the light. I saw his face flush. As though he knew he was being watched he threw a furtive glance toward the door, then shoved the stuff back in the envelope and put it in his side pocket.

I ducked back in the corridor while he went out the door, waited until it closed then snapped the light on and stepped over the junk. One quick look at the papers he had found in the envelope told me what it was. This will was made out only a few months ago, and it left three-quarters of his estate to Ruston and one-quarter to Alice. York had cut the rest out with a single buck.

Junior Ghent had something more important, though. I folded the will into my pocket and ran to the door. I didn't want my little pal to get away.

He didn't. Fifty yards up the drive he was getting the life beat out of him.

I heard his muffled screams, and other voices, too. I got the .45 in my hand and thumbed the safety off and made a dash for them.

Maybe I should have stayed on the grass, but I didn't have that much time. Two figures detached themselves from the one on the ground and broke for the trees. I let one go over their heads that echoed over the grounds like the rolling of thunder, but neither stopped. They went across a clearing and I put on speed to get free of the brush line so I could take aim. Junior stopped that. I tripped over his sprawled figure and went flat on my kisser. The pair scrambled over the wall before I was up. From the ground I tried a snap shot that went wild. On the other side of the wall a car roared into life and shot down the road.

A woman's quick, sharp scream split the air like a knife and caught me flat-footed. Everything happened at once. Briars ripped at my clothes when I went through the brush and whipped at my face. Lights went on in the house and Harvey's voice rang out for help. By the time I reached the porch Billy was standing beside the door in his pajamas.

"Upstairs, Mike, it's Miss Malcom. Somebody shot her!"

Harvey was waving frantically, pointing to her room. I raced inside. Roxy was lying on the floor with blood making a bright red picture on the shoulder of her nightgown. Harvey stood over me, shaking with fear as I ripped the cloth away. I breathed with relief. The bullet had only passed through the flesh under her arm.

I carried her to bed and called to the butler over my shoulder. "Get some hot water and bandages. Get a doctor up here."

Harvey said, "Yes, sir," and scurried away.

Billy came in. "Can I do anything, Mike? I . . . I don't want to be alone."

"Okay, stay with her. I want to see the kid."

I opened the door to Ruston's room and turned on the light. He was sitting up, holding himself erect with his hands, his eyes were fixed on the wall in a blank stare, his mouth open. He never saw me. I shook him, he was stiff as a board, every muscle in his body as rigid as a piece of steel. He jerked convulsively once or twice, never taking his eyes from the wall. It took a lot of force to pull his arms up and straighten him out.

"Harvey, did you call that doctor?"

Billy sang out, "He's doing it now, Mike."

"Damn it, tell him to hurry. The kid's having a fit or something."

He hollered down the stairs to Harvey; I could hear the excited stuttering over the telephone, but it would be awhile before a medic would reach the house. Ruston began to tremble, his eyes rolled back in his head. Leaning over I slapped him sharply across the cheek.

"Ruston, snap out of it," I slapped him again. "Ruston."

This time his eyelids flickered, he came back to normal with a sob. His mouth twitched and he covered his face with his hands. Suddenly he sat up in bed and shouted, "Mike!"

"I'm right here, kid," I said, "take it easy." His face found mine and he reached for my hand. He

126

was trembling from head to foot, his body bathed in cold sweat.

"Miss Malcom . . . ?"

"Is all right," I answered. "She just got a good scare, that's all." I didn't want to frighten him anymore than he was. "Did someone come in here?"

He squeezed my hand. "No . . . there was a noise, and Miss Malcom screamed. Mike, I'm not very brave at all. I'm scared."

The kid had a right to be. "It was nothing. Cover up and be still. I'll be in the next room. Want me to leave the door open?"

"Please, Mike."

I left the light on and put a rubber wedge under the door to keep it open. Billy was standing by the bed holding a handkerchief to Roxy's shoulder. I took it away and looked at it. Not much of a wound, the bullet was of small caliber and had gone in and come out clean. Billy poked me and pointed to the window. The pane had spider-webbed into a thousand cracks with a neat hole at the bottom a few inches above the sill. Tiny glass fragments winked up from the floor. The shot had come in from below, traveling upward. Behind me in the wall was the bullet hole, a small puncture head high. I dug out the slug from the plaster and rolled it over in my hand. A neat piece of lead whose shape had hardly been deformed by the wall, caliber .32. York's gun had found its way home.

I tucked it in my watch pocket. "Stay here, Billy,

I'll be right back."

"Where are you going?" He didn't like me to leave.

"I got a friend downstairs."

Junior was struggling to his feet when I reached him. I helped him with a fist in his collar. This little twerp had a lot of explaining to do. He was a sorry-looking sight. Pieces of gravel were imbedded in the flesh of his face and blood matted the hair of his scalp. One lens of his specs was smashed. I watched him while he detached his lower lip from his teeth, swearing incoherently. The belting he took had left him half-dazed, and he didn't try to resist at all when I walked him toward the house.

When I sat him in a chair he shook his head, touching the cut on his temple. He kept repeating a four-letter word over and over until realization of what had happened hit him. His head came up and I thought he was going to spit at me.

"You got it!" he said accusingly on the verge of tears now.

"Got what?" I leaned forward to get every word. His eyes narrowed.

Junior said sullenly, "Nothing."

Very deliberately I took his tie in my hand and pulled it. He tried to draw back, but I held him close. "Little chum," I said, "you are in a bad spot, very bad. You've been caught breaking and entering. You stole something from York's private hideaway and Miss Malcom has been shot. If you know what's good for you, you'll talk."

"Shot . . . killed?"

There was no sense letting him know the truth. "She's not dead yet. If she dies you're liable to face a murder charge."

"No. No. I didn't do it. I admit I was in the laboratory, but I didn't shoot her. I . . . I didn't get a chance to. Those men jumped on me. I fought for my life."

"Did you? Were you really unconscious? Maybe. I went after them until I heard Miss Malcom scream. Did she scream because you shot her, then faked being knocked out all the while?"

He turned white. A little vein in his forehead throbbed, his hands tightened until his nails drew blood from the palms. "You can't pin it on me," he said. "I didn't do it, I swear."

"No? What did you take from the room back there?"

A pause, then, "Nothing."

I reached for his pockets, daring him to move. Each one I turned inside out, dumping their contents around the bottom of the chair. A wallet, theater stubs, two old letters, some keys and fifty-five cents in change. That was all.

"So somebody else wanted what you found, didn't they?" He didn't answer. "They got it, too."

"I didn't have anything," he repeated.

He was lying through his teeth. "Then why did they wait for you and beat your brains out? Answer that one." He was quiet. I took the will out and waved it at him. "It went with this. It was more important than this, though. But what would be more important to you than a will? You're stupid, Junior. You aren't in this at all, are you? If you had sense enough to burn it you might have come into big dough when the estate was split up, especially with the kid under age. But no, you didn't care whether the will was found and probated or not, because the other thing was more important. It meant more money. How, Junior, how?"

For my little speech I had a sneer thrown at me. "All right," I told him, "I'll tell you what I'm going to do. Right now you look like hell, but you're beautiful compared to what you'll look like in ten minutes. I'm going to slap the crap out of you until you talk. Yell all you want to, it won't do any good."

I pulled back my hand. Junior didn't wait, he started speaking. "Don't. It was nothing. I . . . I stole some money from my uncle once. He caught me and made me sign a statement. I didn't want it to be found or I'd never get a cent. That was it."

"Yes? What made it so important that someone else would want it?"

"I don't know. There was something else attached to the statement that I didn't look at. Maybe they wanted that."

It could have been a lie, but I wasn't sure. What he said made sense. "Did you shoot Miss Malcom?"

"That's silly." I tightened up on the tie again. "Please, you're choking me. I didn't shoot anyone.

130

I never saw her. You can tell, the police have a test haven't they?"

"Yes, a paraffin test. Would you submit to it?"

Relief flooded his face and he nodded. I let him go. If he had pulled the trigger he wouldn't be so damn anxious. Besides, I knew for sure that he hadn't been wearing gloves.

A car pulled up outside and Harvey admitted a short, stout man carrying the bag of his profession. They disappeared upstairs. I turned to Junior. "Get out of here, but stay where you can be reached. If you take a powder I'll squeeze your skinny neck until you turn blue. Remember one thing, if Miss Malcom dies you're it, see, so you better start praying."

He shot out of the chair and half ran for the door. I heard his feet pounding down the drive. I went upstairs.

"How is she?" The doctor applied the last of the tape over the compress and turned.

"Nothing serious. Fainted from shock." He put his instruments back in his bag and took out a notebook. Roxy stirred and woke up.

"Of course you know I'll have to report this. The police must have a record of all gunshot wounds. Her name, please."

Roxy watched me from the bed. I passed it to her. She murmured, "Helen Malcom."

"Address?"

"Here." She gave her age and the doctor noted

a general description then asked me if I had found the bullet.

"Yeah, it was in the wall. A .32 lead-nose job. I'll give it to the police." He snapped the book shut and stuck it in his bag. "I'd like you to see the boy, too, Doctor," I mentioned. "He was in a bad way."

Briefly, I went over what had happened the past few days. The doctor picked his bag up and followed me inside. "I know the boy," he said. "Too much excitement is bad for any youngster, particularly one as finely trained as he is."

"You've seen him before? I thought his father was his doctor."

"Not the boy. However I had occasion to speak to his father several times in town and he spoke rather proudly of his son."

"I should imagine. Here he is."

The doctor took his pulse and I winked over his shoulder. Ruston grinned back. While the doctor examined him I sat at the desk and looked at nine-by-twelve photos of popular cowboy actors Ruston had in a folder. He was a genius, but the boy kept coming out around the seams. A few of the books in the lower shelves were current Western novels and some books on American geography in the 1800s. Beside the desk was a used ten-gallon hat and lariat with the crown of the skimmer autographed by Hollywood's foremost heroic cattle hand. I don't know why York didn't let his kid alone to enjoy himself the way boys should. Ruston would rather be a cowboy than a child prodigy any day, I'd bet. He saw me going over his stuff and smiled.

"Were you ever out West, Mike?" he asked.

"I took some training in the desert when I was with Uncle Whiskers."

"Did you ever see a real cowboy?"

"Nope, but I bunked with one for six months. He used to wear high-heeled boots until the sergeant cracked down on him. Some card. Wanted to wear his hat in the shower. First thing he'd do when he'd get up in the morning was to put on his hat. He couldn't get used to one without a six-inch brim and was forever wanting to tip his hat to the Lieutenant instead of saluting."

Ruston chuckled. "Did he carry a six-shooter?"

"Naw, but he was a dead shot. He could pick the eyes out of a beetle at thirty yards."

The doctor broke up our chitchat by handing the kid some pills. He filled a box with them, printed the time to take them on the side and dashed off a prescription. He handed it to me. "Have this filled. One teaspoonful every two hours for twenty-four hours. There's nothing wrong with him except a slight nervous condition. I'll come back tomorrow to see Miss Malcom again. If her wound starts bleeding call me at once. I gave them both a sedative so they should sleep well until morning."

"Okay, Doctor, thanks." I gave him over to Harvey who ushered him to the door.

Roxy forced a smile. "Did you get them, Mike?"

"Forget about it," I said. "How did you get in the way?"

"I heard a gun go off and turned on the light. I guess I shouldn't have done that. I ran to the window but with the light on I couldn't see a thing. The next thing I knew something hit me in the shoulder. I didn't realize it was a bullet until I saw the hole in the window. That's when I screamed," she added sheepishly.

"I don't blame you, I'd scream too. Did you see the flash of the gun?"

Her head shook on the pillow. "I heard it I think, but it sounded sort of far off. I never dreamed . . ."

"You weren't hurt badly, that's one thing."

"Ruston, how . . ."

"Okay. You scared the hell out of him when you yelled. He's had too much already. That set him off. He was stiff as a fence post when I went in to him."

The sedative was beginning to take effect. Roxy's eyes closed sleepily. I whispered to Billy, "Get me a broom handle or something long and straight, will you?"

He went out and down the corridor. While I waited I looked at the hole the bullet had made, and in my mind pictured where Roxy had stood when she was shot. Billy came in with a long brass tube.

"Couldn't find a broom, but would this curtain rod do?"

"Fine," I said softly. Roxy was asleep now.

"Stand over here by the window."

"What you going to do?"

"Figure out where that shot came from."

I had him hold the rod under his armpit and I sighted along the length of it, lining the tube up with the hole in the wall and the one in the window. This done I told him to keep it that way then threw the window up. More pieces of glass tinkled to the floor. I moved around behind him and peered down the rod.

I was looking at the base of the wall about where the two assailants had climbed the top. That put Junior out of it by a hundred feet. The picture was changing again, nothing balanced. It was like trying to make a mural with a kaleidoscope. Hell's bells. Neither of those two had shot at me, yet that was where the bullet came from. A silencer maybe? A wild shot at someone or a shot carefully aimed. With a .32 it would take an expert to hit the window from that range much less Roxy behind it. Or was the shot actually aimed at her?

"Thanks, Billy, that's all."

He lowered the rod and I shut the window. I called him to one side, away from the bed. "What is it, Mike?"

"Look, I want to think. How about you staying up here in the kid's room tonight. We'll fix some chair cushions up on the floor."

"Okay, if you say so."

"I think it will be best. Somebody will have to keep an eye on them in case they wake up, and Ruston has to take his medicine," I looked at the box, "every three hours. I'll give Harvey the prescription to be filled. Do you mind?"

"No, I think I'll like it here better'n the room downstairs."

"Keep the doors locked."

"And how. I'll push a chair up against them too."

I laughed. "I don't think there will be any more trouble for a while."

His face grew serious. "You can laugh, you got a rod under your arm."

"I'll leave it here for you if you want."

"Not me, Mike. One more strike and I'm out. If I get caught within ten feet of a heater they'll toss me in the clink. I'd sooner take my chances."

He began pulling the cushions from the chairs and I went out. Behind me the lock clicked and a chair went under the knob. Billy wasn't kidding. Nobody was going to get in there tonight.

Chapter Seven

Downstairs I dialed the operator and asked for the highway patrol. She connected me with headquarters and a sharp voice crackled at me. "Sergeant Price, please."

"He's not here right now, is there a message?"

"Yeah, this is Mike Hammer. Tell him that Miss Malcom, the York kid's nurse, was shot through the shoulder by a thirty-two-caliber bullet. Her condition isn't serious and she'll he able to answer questions in the morning. The shot was fired from somewhere on the grounds but the one who fired it escaped."

"I got it. Anything else?"

"Yes, but I'll give it to him in person. Have they found any trace of Grange yet?"

"They picked up her hat along the shore of the inlet. Sergeant Price told me to tell you if you called."

"Thanks. They still looking for her?"

"A boat's grappling the mouth of the channel right now."

"Okay, if I get time I'll call back later." The cop thanked me and hung up. Harvey waited to see whether I was going out or not, and when

I headed for the door got my hat.

"Will you be back tonight, sir?"

"I don't know. Lock the door anyway."

"Yes, sir."

I tooled my car up the drive and honked for Henry to come out and open the gates. Although there was a light on in his cottage, Henry didn't appear. I climbed out again and walked in the place. The gatekeeper was sound asleep in his chair, a paper folded across his lap.

After I shook him and swore a little his eyes opened, but not the way a waking person's do. They were heavy and dull, he was barely able to raise his head. The shock of seeing me there did more to put some life in him than the shaking. He blinked a few times and ran his hand over his forehead.

"I'm . . . sorry, sir. Can't understand myself . . . lately. These awful headaches, and going to sleep like that."

"What's the matter with you, Henry?"

"It's . . . nothing, sir. Perhaps it's the aspirin." He pointed to a bottle of common aspirin tablets on the table. I picked it up and looked at the label. A well-known brand. I looked again, then shook some out on my palm. There were no manufacturer's initials on the tablets at all. There were supposed to be, I used enough of them myself.

"Where did you get these, Henry?"

"Mr. York gave them to me last week. I had several fierce headaches. The aspirin relieved me."

"Did you take these the night of the kidnapping?"

His eyes drifted to mine, held. "Why, yes. Yes, I did."

"Better lay off them. They aren't good for you. Did you hear anything tonight?"

"No, I don't believe I did. Why?"

"Oh, no reason. Mind if I take some of these with me?" He shook his head and I pocketed a few tablets. "Stay here," I said, "I'll open the gates."

Henry nodded and was asleep before I left the room. That was why the kidnapper got in so easily. That was why York left and the killer left and I left without being heard at the gate.

It was a good bet that someone substituted sleeping tablets for the aspirins. Oh, brother, the killer was getting cuter all the time.

But the pieces were coming together one by one. They didn't fit the slots, but they were there, ready to be assembled as soon as someone said the wrong word, or made a wrong move. The puzzle was closer to the house now, but it was outside, too. Who wanted Henry to be asleep while Ruston was snatched? Who wanted it so bad that his habits were studied and sleeping pills slipped into his aspirin bottle? If someone was that thorough they could have given him something to cause the headaches to start with. And who was in league with that person on the outside?

A wrong move or a wrong word. Someone would slip sometime. Maybe they just needed a little push. I had Junior where the hair was short now, that meant I had the old lady, too. Jump the fence to the other side now. Alice. She said *tsk, tsk* when I told them York was dead. Sweet thing.

I had to make another phone call to trooper headquarters to collect the list of addresses from the statements. Price still hadn't come in, but evidently he had passed the word to give me any help I needed, for there was no hesitation about handing me the information.

Alice lived west of town in a suburb called Wooster. It was little less than a crossroad off the main highway, but from the size of the mansions that dotted the estates it was a refuge of the wealthy. The town itself boasted a block of storefronts whose windows showed nothing but the best. Above each store was an apartment. The bricks were white, the metal work bright and new. There was an aura of dignity and pomp in the way they nestled there. Alice lived above the fur shop, two stores from the end.

I parked between a new Ford and a Caddy convertible. There were no lights on in Alice's apartment, but I didn't doubt that she'd want to see me. I slid out and went into the tiny foyer and looked at the bell. It was hers. For a good five seconds I held my finger on it, then opened the door and went up the steps. Before I reached the top, Alice, in the last stages of closing her robe, opened the door, sending a shaft of light in my face.

"Well, I'll be damned," she exclaimed. "You

certainly pick an awful time to visit your friends."

"Aren't you glad to see me?" I grinned.

"Silly, come on in. Of course I'm glad to see you."

"I hate to get you up like this."

"You didn't. I was lying in bed reading, that's all." She paused just inside the door. "This isn't a professional visit, is it?"

"Hardly. I finally got sick and tired of the whole damn setup and decided to give my mind a rest."

She shut the door. "Kiss me."

I pecked her on the nose. "Can't I even take my hat off?"

"Oooo," she gasped, "the way you said that!"

I dropped my slicker and hat on a rack by the door and trailed her to the living room. "Have a drink?" she asked me.

I made with three fingers together. "So much, and ginger."

When she went for the ice I took the place in with a sweep of my head. Swell, strictly swell. It was better than the best Park Avenue apartment I'd ever been in, even if it was above a store. The furniture cost money and the oils on the wall even more. There were books and books, first editions and costly manuscripts. York had done very well by his niece.

Alice came back with two highballs in her hand. "Take one," she offered. I picked the big one. We toasted silently, she with the devil in her eyes, and drank.

"Good?"

I bobbed my head. "Old stuff, isn't it?"

"Over twenty years. Uncle Rudy gave it to me." She put her drink down and turned off the overhead lights, switching on a shaded table lamp instead. From a cabinet she selected an assortment of records and put them in the player. "Atmosphere," she explained impishly.

I didn't see why we needed it. When she had the lamp at her back the robe became transparent enough to create its own atmosphere. She was all woman, this one, bigger than I thought. Her carriage was seduction itself and she knew it. The needle came down and soft Oriental music filled the room. I closed my eyes and visualized women in scarlet veils dancing for the sultan. The sultan was me. Alice said something I didn't catch and left.

When she came back she was wearing the cobwebs. Nothing else.

"You aren't too tired tonight?"

"Not tonight," I said.

She sat down beside me. "I think you were faking the last time, and after all my trouble."

Her skin was soft and velvety-looking under the cobwebs, a vein in her throat pulsed steadily. I let my eyes follow the contours of her shoulders and down her body. Impertinent breasts that mocked my former hesitance, a flat stomach waiting for the touch to set off the fuse, thighs that wanted no part of shielding cloth.

I had difficulty getting it out. "I *had* to be tired."

She crossed her legs, the cobwebs parted. "Or crazy," she added.

I finished the drink off in a hurry and held out the glass for another. I needed something to steady my nerves.

Ice clinked, glass rang against glass. She measured the whisky and poured it in. This time she pulled the coffee table over so she wouldn't have to get up again. The record changed and the gentle strains of a violin ran through the *Hungarian Rhapsody*. Alice moved closer to me. I could feel the warmth of her body through my clothes. The drinks went down. When the record changed again she had her head on my shoulder.

"Have you been working hard, Mike?"

"No, just legwork."

Her hair brushed my face; soft, lovely hair that smelled of jasmine. "Do you think they'll find her?"

I stroked her neck, letting my fingers bite in just a little. "I think so. Sidon is too small a town to try to hide in. Did you know her well?"

"Ummm. What? Oh, no. She was very distant to all of us."

More jasmine. She buried her face in my shoulder. "You're a thing yourself," I grinned. "Shouldn't you be wearing black?"

"No. It doesn't become me."

I blew in her ear. "No respect for the dead."

"Uncle never liked all those post-funeral displays anyway."

"Well, you should do something since you were

his favorite niece. He left you a nice lump of cash."

She ran her fingers through my hair, bending my head close to hers. "Did he?" Lightly, her tongue ran over her lips, a pink, darting temptation.

"Uh-huh." We rubbed noses, getting closer all the time. "I saw his will. He must have liked you."

"Just you like me, Mike, that's all I want." Her mouth opened slightly. I couldn't take anymore. I grabbed her in my arms and crushed her lips against mine. She was a living heartbeat, an endless fire that burned hot and deep. Her arms went about me, holding tightly. Once, out of sheer passion, she bit me like a cat would bite.

She tore her mouth away and pressed it against my neck, then rubbed her shoulders from side to side against my chest until the cobwebs slipped down her arms and pinioned them there. I touched her flesh, bruised her until she moaned in painful ecstasy, demanding more. Her fingers fumbled with the buttons of my coat. Somehow I got it off and draped it over a chair, then she started on my tie. "So many clothes, Mike, you have so many clothes." She kissed me again.

"Carry me inside." I scooped her off the couch, cradling her in my arms, the cobwebs trailing beneath her. She pointed with her finger, her eyes almost closed. "In there."

No lights. The comforter was cool and fluffy. She told me to stay there and kissed my eyes shut. I felt her leave the bed and go into the living room. The record changed and a louder piece sent notes

144

of triumph cascading into the room. Agonising minutes passed waiting until she returned, bearing two half-full glasses on a tray like a gorgeous slave girl. Gone now were even the cobwebs.

"To us, Mike, and this night." We drank. She came to me with arms outstretched. The music came and went, piece after piece, but we heard nothing nor cared. Then there was no sound at all except the breathing.

It was well into morning before we stirred. Alice said no, but I had to leave. She coaxed, but now the sight of her meant less and I could refuse. I found my shoes, laced them, and tucked the covers under her chin.

"Kiss me." She held her mouth up.

"No."

"Just one?"

"All right, just one." She wasn't making it any too easy. I pushed her back against the pillows and said good night.

"You're so ugly, Mike. So ugly you're beautiful."

"Thanks, so are you." I waved and left her. In the living room I picked my coat up from the floor and dusted it off. My aim was getting worse, I thought I had it on the chair.

On the way out I dropped the night latch and shut the door softly. Alice, lovely, lovely Alice. She had a body out of this world. I ran down the stairs pulling on my slicker. Outside the sheen of the rain glimmered from the streets. I gave the brim of my hat a final tug and stepped out.

There were no flashes of light, no final moments of distortion. Simply that one sickening, hollow-sounding smash on the back of the head and the sidewalk came up and hit me in the face.

I was sick. It ran down my chin and wet my shirt. The smell of it made me sicker. My head was a huge balloon that kept getting bigger and bigger until it was taut and ready to burst into a thousand fragments. Something cold and metallic jarred my face repeatedly. I was cramped, horribly cramped. Even when I tried to move I stayed cramped. Ropes bit into my wrists leaving hempen splinters imbedded under the skin, burning like darts. Whenever the car hit a bump the jack on the floor would slam into my nose.

No one else was with me back there. The empty shoulder holster bit into my side. Nice going, I thought, you walked into that with your mouth open and your eyes shut. I tried to see over the back of the seat, but I couldn't raise myself that far. We turned off the smooth concrete of the highway and the roadway became sloshy and irregular. The jack bounced around more often. First I tried to hold it down with my forehead, but it didn't work, then I drew back from it. That was worse. The muscles in my back ached with the torture of the rack.

I got mad as hell. Sucker. That's what I was. Sucker. Someone was taking me for a damn newcomer at this racket. Working me over with a billy then tossing me in the back of a car. Just like the prohibition days, going for a ride. What the hell did I look like? I had been tied up before and I had been in the back of a car before, but I didn't stay there long. After the first time I learned my lesson. Boy Scout stuff, be prepared. Some son of a bitch was going to get his brains kicked out.

The car skidded to a stop. The driver got out and opened the door. His hands went under my armpits and I was thrown into the mud. Feet straddled me, feet that merged into a dark overcoat and a masked face, and a hand holding my own gun so that I was looking down the muzzle.

"Where is it?" the guy said. His voice carried an obvious attempt at disguise.

"What are you talking about?"

"Damn you anyway, what did you do with it? Don't try to stall me, what did you do with it? You hid it somewhere, you bastard, it wasn't in your pocket. Start talking or I'll shoot your head off!"

The guy was working himself up into a kill-crazy mood. "How do I know where it is if you won't tell me what you want," I snarled.

"All right, you bastard, get smart. You stuck your neck out once too often. I'll show you." He stuck the gun in his pocket and bent over, his hands fastening in my coat collar and under my arm. I didn't help him any. I gave him damn near two hundred pounds of dead weight to drag into the trees.

Twice the guy snagged himself in the brush and half-fell. He took it out on me with a slap in the head and a nasty boot in the ribs. Every once in a while he'd curse and get a better grip on my coat, muttering under his breath what was going to happen to me. Fifty yards into the woods was enough. He dropped me in a heap and dragged the rod out again, fighting for his breath. The guy knew guns. The safety was off and the red was ready to spit.

"Say it. Say it now, damn you, or you'll never say it. What did you do with them . . . or should I work you over first?"

"Go to hell, you pig."

His hand went up quickly. The gun described a chopping arc toward my jaw. That was what I was waiting for. I grabbed the gun with both hands and yanked, twisting at the same time. He screamed when his shoulder jumped out of the socket, screamed again when I clubbed the edge of my palm against his neck.

Feet jabbed out and ripped into my side, he scrambled to get up. In the middle of it I lost the gun. I held on with one arm and sank my fist into him, but the power of the blow was lost in that awkward position.

But it was enough. He wrenched away, regained his feet and went scrambling through the underbrush. By the time I found the gun he was gone. Time again. If I had had only a minute more I could have chased him, but I hadn't had time to cut my feet loose. Yeah, I'd been on the floor of a car before with my hands tied behind my back. After that first time I have always carried a safety-razor blade slipped through the open seam into the double layer of cloth under my belt. It works nice, very handy. Someday I'd get tied up with my hands in front and I'd be stuck.

The knots were soft. A few minutes with them and I was on my feet. I tried to follow his tracks a few yards, but gave it up as a bad job. He had fallen into a couple of soft spots and left hunks of his clothes hanging on some tree limbs. He didn't know where he was going and didn't care. All he knew was that if he stopped and I caught him he'd die in that swamp as sure as he was born. It was almost funny. I turned around and waded back through the tangled underbrush, dodging snaky low-hanging branches that tried to whip my eyes out.

At least I had the car. My erstwhile friend was going to have to hoof it back to camp. I walked around the job, a late Chevvy sedan. The glove compartment was empty, the interior in need of a cleaning. Wrapped around the steering post was the ownership card with the owner's name: Mrs. Margaret Murphy, age fifty-two, address in Wooster, occupation, cook. A hell of a note, lifting some poor servant's buggy. I started it up. It would be back in town before it was missed.

When I turned around I plowed through the ruts of a country road for five minutes before reaching the main highway. My lights hit a sign pointing north to Wooster. I must have been out

149

some time, it was over fifteen miles to the city. Once on the concrete I stepped on the gas. More pieces of the puzzle. I had something. I felt in my pocket; the later will was still there. Then what the hell was it? What was so almighty important that I'd been taken for a ride and threatened to make me talk?

Ordinarily I'm not stupid, on the contrary, my mind can pick up threads and weave them into whole cloth, but now I felt like putting on the dunce cap and sitting in the corner.

Nuts.

Twenty minutes to nine I was on the outskirts of Wooster. I turned down the first side street I came to, parked and got out of the car after wiping off any prints I might have made. I didn't know just how the local police operated, but I wasn't in the mood to do any explaining. I picked up the main road again and strode uphill toward Alice's. If she was up there was no indication of it. I recovered my hat from the foyer, cast one look up to the shuttered window and got in my own car. Things were breaking all around my head and I couldn't make any sense out of anything. It was like taking an exam with the answer sheet in front of you and failing because you forgot your glasses.

Going back to Sidon I had time to think. No traffic, just the steady hum of the engine and the sharp whirr of the tires. I was supposed to have something. I didn't have it. Yet certain parties were so sure I did have it they put the buzz on me. *It, it,* for Pete's sake, why don't they name the name? I had two wills and some ideas. They didn't want the wills and they didn't know about the ideas. Something else I might have picked up . . . or didn't pick up.

Of course. Of all the potted, tin-headed fools, I took the cake. Junior Ghent got more than the one will. That was all he had left after the two boys got done with him. They took something else, but whatever it was Junior didn't want me messing in his plans by telling me about it. They took it all right, but somewhere between me and the wall they dropped that important something, and figuring me to be smarter than I should have been, thought I must have found it.

I grinned at myself in the rearview mirror. I'm thick sometimes, but hit me often enough and I get the idea. I didn't even have to worry about Junior beating me to it. He *knew* they had it . . . he wouldn't plan on them dropping it. My curiosity was getting tired of thinking in terms of *its.* This had better be good or I was going to be pretty teed off.

Nice, sweet little case. Two hostile camps. Both fighting each other, both fighting me. In between a lot of people getting shot at and Ruston kidnapped to boot. Instead of a logical starting place it traveled in circles. I kicked the gas pedal a little harder.

Harvey was waiting with the door open when I turned up the drive. I waved him inside and followed the gravel drive to the spot where Junior had taken his shellacking. After a few false starts, I picked out the trail the two had taken across the yard and began tracking. Here and there a footprint was still visible in the soft sod; a twig broken off, flower stalks bent, a stone kicked aside. I let my eyes read over every inch of the path and six feet to the sides, too. If I knew what I was looking for it wouldn't have been so bad. As it was, it took me a good twenty minutes to reach the wall.

That was where it was. Lying face up in full view of anybody who cared to look. A glaring white patch against the shrubbery, a slightly crinkled, but still sealed envelope.

The IT.

Under my fingers I felt a handful of what felt like postcards. With a shrug I shoved the envelope unopened into my pocket. Item one. I poked around in the grass and held the shrubs aside with my feet. Nothing. I got down on the ground and looked across the grass at a low angle, hoping to catch the sunlight glinting off metal. The rough calculations I took from Roxy's room showed this to be the point of origin of the bullet, but nowhere could I see an empty shell. Hell, it could have been a revolver, then there would be no ejected shell. Or it could have been another gun instead of York's. Nuts there. A .32 is a defensive weapon. Anybody who wants to kill uses a .38 or better, especially at that range. I checked the distance to Roxy's window again. Just to hit the house would mean an elevation of thirty degrees. The lad who made the window was good. Better than that, he was perfect. Only he must have fired from a hole in the ground, because there was no place he could have hidden in this area. That is, if it wasn't one of the two who went over the wall.

I gave up and went back to the car and drove around to the front of the house.

Dutiful Harvey stared at the dirt on my clothes and said, "There's been an accident, sir?"

"You might call it that," I agreed pleasantly. "How is Miss Malcom?"

"Fine, sir. The doctor was here this morning and said she was not in any danger at all."

"The boy?"

"Still quite agitated after his experience. The doctor gave him another sedative. Parks has remained with them all this while. He hasn't set foot out of the room since you left."

"Good. Has anyone been here at all?"

"No, sir. Sergeant Price called several times and wants you to call him back."

"Okay, Harvey, thanks. Think you can find me something to eat? I'm starved."

"Certainly, sir."

I trotted upstairs and knocked on the door. Billy's voice cautiously inquired who it was, and when I answered pulled a chair away from the door and unlocked it.

"Hi, Billy."

"Hello, Mike . . . what the hell happened?"

"Somebody took me for a ride."

"Cripes, don't be so calm about it."

153

"Why not? The other guy has to walk back."

"Who?"

"I don't know yet."

Roxy was grinning at me from the bed. "Come over and kiss me, Mike." I gave her a playful tap on the jaw.

"You heal fast."

"I'll do better if you kiss me." I did. Her mouth was a field of burning poppies.

"Okay?"

"I want more."

"When you get better." I squeezed her hand. Before I went into Ruston's room I dusted myself off in front of the mirror. He had heard me come in and was all smiles.

"Hello, Mike. Can you stay here awhile this time?"

"Oh, maybe. Feeling good?"

"I feel all right, but I've been in bed too long. My back is tired."

"I think you'll be able to get up today. I'll have Billy take you for a stroll around the house. I'd do it myself only I have some work to clean up."

"Mike . . . how is everything coming? I mean . . ."

"Don't think about it, Ruston."

"That's all I can do when I lie here awake. I keep thinking of that night, and Dad and Miss Grange. If only there was something I could do I'd feel better."

"The best you can do is stay right here until everything's settled."

"I read in books . . . they were books of no account . . . but sometimes in cases like this the police used the victim as bait. That is, they exposed a person to the advantage of the criminal to see if the criminal would make another attempt. Do you think . . ."

"I think you have a lot of spunk to suggest a thing like that, but the answer is no. You aren't being the target for another snatch, not if I can help it. There're too many other ways. Now how about you hopping into your clothes and getting that airing." I peeled the covers back and helped him out of bed. For a few seconds he was a bit unsteady, but he settled down with a grin and went to the closet. I called Billy in and told him what to do. Billy wasn't too crazy about the idea, but it being daylight, and since I said that I'd stick around, he agreed.

I left the two of them there, winked at Roxy and went downstairs in time to lift a pair of sandwiches and a cup of coffee from Harvey's tray. Grunting my thanks through a mouthful of food I went into the living room and parked in the big chair. For the first time since I had been there a fire blazed away in the fireplace. Good old Harvey. I wolfed down the first sandwich and drowned it in coffee. Only then did I take the envelope out of my pocket. The flap was pasted on crooked, so it had to be the morning dew that had held it shut. I remembered that look on Junior's face when he had seen what was in it. I wondered if *it* was so good mine would look the same way.

I ran my finger under the flap and drew out six pictures.

Now I saw why Junior got so excited. Of the two women in the photos, the only clothes in evidence were shoes. And Myra Grange only had one on at that. Mostly, she wore a leer. A big juicy leer. Alice Nichols looked expectant. The pictures were pornography of the worst sort. Six of them, every one different, both parties fully recognizable, yet the views were of a candid sort, not deliberately posed. No, that wasn't quite it, they were posed, yet unposed . . . at least Myra Grange wasn't posing.

I had to study the shots a good ten minutes before I got the connection. What I had taken to be a border around the pictures done in the printing was really part of the shot. These pics were taken with a hidden camera, one concealed behind a dresser, with the supposed border being some books that did the concealing. A hidden camera and a time arrangement to trip it every so often.

No, Myra Grange wasn't posing, but Alice Nichols was. She had deliberately maneuvered for position each time so Grange was sure to be in perfect focus.

How nice, Alice. How very nicely you and York framed Grange. A frame to neutralize another frame. So?

I fired up a butt and shoved the pics back in my pocket. The outer rim of the puzzle was falling into the grooves in my mind now. Grange had an old will. Why? Would York have settled his entire estate on her voluntarily? Or could he have been forced into it? If Grange had something on her boss . . . something big . . . it had to be big . . . then she could call the squeeze play, and be reasonably sure of making a touchdown, especially when York didn't have long to go anyway. But sometime later York had found out about Grange and her habits and saw a way out. Damn, it was making sense now. He played up to Rhoda Ghent, plied her with gifts, then asked her to proposition Grange. She refused and he dropped her like a hot potato then started on Alice. York should have talked to her first. Alice had no inhibitions anyway, and a cut of York's will meant plenty of action to her. She makes eyes at Grange, Grange makes eyes at Alice and the show is on with the lights properly fed and the camera in position. Alice hands York the negatives, York has a showdown with Grange, threatening to make the pictures public and Grange folds up, yet holds onto the old will in the hope something would happen to make York change his mind. Something like a meat cleaver perhaps? It tied in with what Roxy told me. It could even explain the big play after the pictures. Junior had found out about them some-how, possibly from his sister. If he could get the shots in a law court he could prove how Alice came by her share and get her kicked right out of the show. At least then the family might have some chance to split the quarter of the estate. One hostile camp taken care of. Alice had to be the other. She had to have the pictures before Junior could get them . . . or anybody else for that matter. What could be better than promising a future split of her quarter if they agreed to get the pictures for her? That fit, too. Except that they came too late and saw Junior, knew that he had beaten them to it, so they waylay him, take the stuff and blow. Only I happened in at the wrong time and in the excitement the package gets lost.

I dragged heavily on the cigarette and ran over it again, checking every detail. It stayed the same way. I liked it. Billy and Ruston yelled to me on their way out, but I only waved to them. I was trying to reason out what it was that Grange had on York in the beginning to start a snowball as big as this one rolling downhill.

Flames were licking the top of their sooty cavern. Dante's own inferno, hot, roasting, destroying. It would have been so nice if I could only have known what York had hidden in the pillar of the fireplace. York's secret hiding place, that and the chair bottom. Why two places unless he didn't want to have all his eggs in one basket. Or was it another case of first things first? He could have put something in the fireplace years ago and not cared to change it.

With a show of impatience I flipped the remains of the butt into the flames, then stretched my legs out toward the fireplace. Secrets, secrets, so damn many secrets. I moved my head to one side so I could see the brick posts on the end of the smoke-blackened pit. It was well concealed, that cache. Curiosity again. I got up and looked it over more closely. Not a brick out of line, not a seam visible. Unless you saw it open you would never guess it to be there.

I went over every inch of it, rapping the bricks with my bare knuckles, but unlike wood, they gave off no sound. There had to be a trip for it somewhere. I looked again where the stone joined the wall. One place shoulder-high was smudged. I pressed.

The tiny door clicked and swung open.

Nice. It was faced with whole brick that joined with a fit in a recess of the concrete that the eye couldn't discern. To get my hand in I had to hold the door open against the force of a spring. I fished around, but felt nothing except cold masonry until I went to take my hand out. A piece of paper caught in the hinge mechanism brushed my fingers. I worked it out slowly, because at the first attempt to dislodge it, part of the paper crumbled to dust. When I let the door go it snapped shut, and I was holding a piece of an ancient newspaper.

It was brown with age, ready to fall apart at the slightest pressure. The print was faded, but legible. It bore the dateline of a New York edition, one that was on the stands October 9, fourteen years ago. What happened fourteen years ago? The rest of the paper had been stolen, this was a piece torn off when it was lifted from the well in the fireplace. A dateline, nothing but a fourteen-year-old dateline.

I'm getting old, I thought. These things ought to make an impression sooner. Fourteen years ago Ruston had been born.

159

Chapter Eight

Somehow, the library had an unused look. An age-less caretaker shuffled up the aisle carrying a broom and a dustpan, looking for something to sweep. The librarian, untrue to type, was busy painting her mouth an unholy red, and never looked up until I rapped on the desk. That got me a quick smile, a fast once-over, then an even bigger smile.

"Good morning. Can I help you?"

"Maybe. Do you keep back copies of New York papers?"

She stood up and smoothed out her dress around her hips where it didn't need smoothing at all. "This way, please."

I followed her at a six-foot interval, enough so I could watch her legs that so obviously wanted watching. They were pretty nice legs. I couldn't blame her a bit for wanting to show them off. We angled around behind ceiling-high book-cases until we came to a stairwell. Legs threw a light switch and took me downstairs. A musty odor of old leather and paper hit me on the last step. Little trickles of moisture beaded the metal bins and left dark stains on the concrete walls.

A hell of a place for books.

"Here they are." She pointed to a tier of shelves, stacked with newspapers, separated by layers of cardboard. Together we located the old *Globe* editions then began peeling off the layers. In ten minutes we both looked like we had been playing in coal. Legs threw me a pout. "I certainly hope that whatever you're after is worth all this trouble."

"It is, honey," I told her, "it is. Keep your eyes open for October 9."

Another five minutes, then, "This it?"

I would have kissed her if she didn't have such a dirty face. "That's the one. Thanks."

She handed it over. I glanced at the dateline, then at the one in my hand. They matched. We laid the paper out on a reading desk and pulled on the overhead light. I thumbed through the leaves, turning them over as I scanned each column. Legs couldn't stand it any longer. "Please . . . what are you looking for?"

I said a nasty word and tapped the bottom of the page. "This."

"But . . ."

"I know. It's gone. Somebody ripped it out."

She said the same nasty word, then asked, "What was it?"

"Beats me, honey. Got any duplicates around?"

"No, we only keep one copy. There's rarely any call for them except from an occasional high-school history student who is writing a thesis on something or other."

"Uh-huh." Tearing that spot out wasn't going

to do any good. There were other libraries. Some-body was trying to stall me for time. Okay, okay, I have all the time in the world. More time than you have, brother.

I helped her stack the papers back on their shelves before going upstairs. We both ducked into washrooms to get years of dust off our skin, only she beat me out. I half expected it anyway.

When we were walking toward the door I dropped a flyer. "Say, do you know Myra Grange?" Her breath caught and held. "Why . . . no. That is, isn't she the one . . . I mean with Mr. York?"

I nodded. She had made a good job of covering up, but I didn't miss that violent blush of emotion that surged into her cheeks at the mention of Grange's name. So this was why the vanishing lady spent so many hours in the library. "The same," I said. "Did she ever go down there?"

"No." A pause. "No, I don't think so. Oh, yes. She did once. She took the boy . . . Mr. York's son down there, but that was when I first came here. I went with them. They looked over some old manuscripts, but that was all."

"When was she here last?"

"Who are you?" She looked scared.

My badge was in my hand. She didn't have to read it. All she needed was the sight of the shield to start shaking. "She was here . . . about a week ago."

Very carefully, I looked at her. "No good. That was too long ago. Let's put it this way. When

162

did you *see* her last?" Legs got the point. She knew I knew about Myra and guessed as much about her. Another blush, only this one faded with the fear behind it.

"A . . . a week ago, I told you." I thanked her and went out. Legs was lying through her teeth and I couldn't blame her.

The water was starting to bubble now. It wouldn't be long before it started to boil. Two things to do before I went to New York, one just for the pleasure of it. I made my first stop at a drugstore. A short, squat pharmacist came out from behind the glass partition and murmured his greetings. I threw the pills I had taken from Henry's bottle on the counter in front of me.

"These were being taken for aspirin," I said. "Can you tell me what they are?"

He looked at me and shrugged, picking up one in his fingers. He touched a cautious tongue to the white surface, then smelled it. "Not aspirin," he told me. "Have you any idea what they might be?"

"I'd say sleeping pills. One of the barbiturates." The druggist nodded and went back behind his glass. I waited perhaps five minutes before he came back again.

"You were right," he said. I threw two five-dollar bills on the counter and scooped up the rest of the pills. Very snazzy, killer, you got a lot of tricks up your sleeve. A very thorough guy. It was going to be funny when I had that killer at the end of my rod. I wondered if he was thorough enough to try to get rid of me.

Back and forth, back and forth. Like a swing. From kidnapping to murder to petty conniving and back to the kidnapping again. Run, run, run. Shuttle train stuff. Too many details. They were like a shroud that the killer was trying to draw around the original motive. That, there had to be. Only it was getting lost in the mess. It could have been an accident, this eruption of pointless crimes, or they might have happened anyway, or they could have been foreseen by the killer and used to his own advantage. No, nobody could be that smart. There's something about crime that's like a disease. It spreads worse than the flu once it gets started. It already had a good start when Ruston was kidnapped. It seemed like that was months ago, but it wasn't . . . just a few short days.

I reviewed every detail on my way to Wooster, but the answer always came up the same. Either I was dumb or the killer was pretty cagey. I had to find Mallory, I had to find Grange, I had to find the killer if he wasn't one of those two. So far all I found was a play behind the curtain.

Halfway there I gave up thinking and concentrated on the road. With every mile I'd gotten madder until I was chain-smoking right through my deck of butts. Wooster was alive this time. People walked along the streets in noisy contentment, limousines blared indignantly at lesser cars in front of them, and a steady stream of traffic went in and out of the shop doors. There was plenty of room in front of Alice's house. I parked the car and went into the foyer, remembering vividly the crack on my skull.

This time the buzz was a short one. I took the stairs fast, but she was faster. She stood in the door with a smile, ready to be kissed. I said, "Hello, Alice," but I didn't kiss her. Her smile broke nervously.

"What's the matter, Mike?"

"Nothing, kid, nothing at all. Why?"

"You look displeased about something." That was putting it mildly.

I went inside without lifting my hat. Alice went to reach for the decanter, but I stopped her by throwing the envelope on the coffee table. "You were looking for these, I think."

"I?" She pulled one of the pictures out of the wrapper, then shoved it back hastily, her face going white. I grinned.

Then I got nasty. "In payment for last night."

"You can go now."

"Uh-uh. Not yet." Her eyes followed mine to the ashtray. There were four butts there, two of them had lipstick on them and the other two weren't my brand.

Alice tried to scream a warning, but it never got past her lips. The back of my hand caught her across the mouth and she rolled into the sofa, gasping with the sting of the blow. I turned on my heels and went to the bedroom and kicked the door open. William Graham was sitting on the edge of the bed as nice as you please smoking a cigarette. His face was scratched in a dozen places and hunks torn out of his clothes from the briars in the woods.

Every bit of color drained out of his skin. I grabbed him before he could stand up and smashed him right in the nose. Blood spurted all over my coat. His arms flailed out, trying to push me away, but I clipped him again on the nose, and again, until there was nothing but a soggy, pulpy mass of flesh to hit. Then I went to work on the rest of his puss. Slapping, punching, then a nasty cut with the side of my hand. He was limp in my grasp, his head thrown back and his eyes wide open. I let him go and he sagged into a shapeless heap on the floor. It was going to take a thousand dollars worth of surgery to make his face the same.

Alice had seen and heard. When I went into the living room she was crouched in terror behind a chair. That didn't stop me. I yanked her out; her dress split down the middle. "Lie to me, Alice," I warned, "and you'll look just like him. Maybe worse. You put him up to bumping me, didn't you?"

All she could do was nod soundlessly.

"You told him he wasn't in the will, but if he and his brother found the pictures and gave them to you you'd cut them in for your share?"

She nodded again. I pushed her back. "York made the will," I said. "It was his dough and I don't care what he did with it. Take your share and go to hell with it. You probably will anyway. Tell Arthur I'll be looking for him. When I find

166

him he's going to look like his brother."

I left her looking eighty years old. William was moaning through his own blood when I went out the door. Good party. I liked it. There would be no more rides from that enemy camp. The redskins have left, vamoosed, departed.

There was only one angle to the Graham boys that I couldn't cover. Which one of them took the shot at Roxy and why? I'll be damned if I heard a shot. They didn't stop long enough to say boo far less than snap off a quickie. And they certainly would have shot at me, not toward the window. I wasn't sure of anything, but if there was money on the table I'd say that neither one had used a gun at all that night. It was details like that that creased me up. I had to make a choice one way or the other and follow it to a conclusion. All right, it was made. The Graham boys were out. Someone else fired it.

New York was a dismal sight after the country. I hadn't thought the grass and the trees with their ugly bilious color of green could have made such an impression on me. Somehow the crowded streets and the endless babble of voices gave me a dirty taste in my mouth. I rolled into a parking lot, pocketed my ticket, then turned into a chain drugstore on the stem. My first call was back to Sidon. Harvey answered and I told him to keep the kid in the room with Roxy and Billy until I got back and take any calls that came for me. My next dime got Pat Chambers, Captain of Homicide.

167

"Greetings, chum," I said, "this is Uncle Mike."

"It's about time you buzzed me. I was beginning to think you cooled off another citizen and were on the fly. Where are you?"

"Right off Times Square."

"Coming down?"

"No, Pat. I have some business to attend to. Look, how about meeting me on the steps of the library. West Forty-third Street entrance. It's important."

"Okay. Say in about half an hour. Will that do?"

I told him fine and hung up. Pat was tops in my book. A careful, crafty cop, and all cop. He looked more like a gentleman-about-town, but there it ended. Pat had a mind like an adding machine and a talent for police work backed up by the finest department in the world. Ordinarily a city cop has no truck with a private eye, but Pat and I had been buddies a long time with one exception. It was a case of mutual respect, I guess.

At a stand-up-and-eat joint I grabbed a couple dogs and a lemonade then beat it to the library in time to see Pat step out of a prowl car. We shook hands and tossed some remarks back and forth before Pat asked, "What's the story?"

"Let's go inside where we can talk."

We went through the two sets of doors and into the reading room. Holding my voice down I said, "Ever hear of Rudolph York, Pat?"

"So?" He had.

I gave him the story in brief, adding at the end, "Now I want to see what was attached to the rest of this dateline. It'll be here somewhere, and it's liable to turn up something you can help me with."

"For instance?"

"I don't know yet, but police records go back pretty far, don't they? What I want to know may have happened fourteen years ago. My memory isn't that good."

"Okay, let's see what we can dig up."

Instead of going through the regular library routine, Pat flashed his shield and we got an escort to where the papers were filed. The old gentleman in the faded blue serge went unerringly to the right bin, pulled out a drawer and selected the edition I wanted all on the first try. He pointed to a table and pulled out chairs for us. My hands were trembling with the excitement of it when I opened the paper.

It was there. Two columns right down the side of the page. Two columns about six-inches long with a photo of York when he was a lot younger. Fourteen years younger. A twenty-four-point heading smacked me between the eyes with its implications.

FATHER ACCUSES SCIENTIST OF BABY SWITCH

Herron Mallory, whose wife gave birth to a seven-pound boy that died two days later, has accused Rudolph York, renowned scientist, of switching babies. Mallory alleged that it was York's son, not his, who died. His claim is based on the fact that he saw his own child soon after birth, and recognized it again when it was shown to York, his own having been pronounced dead earlier. Authorities denied that such a mistake could have happened. Head Nurse, Rita Cambell, verified their denials by assuring both York and Mallory that she had been in complete charge during the two days, and recognized both babies by sight, confirming identification by their bracelets. Mrs. York died during childbirth.

I let out a long, low whistle. The ball had moved up to midfield. Pat suggested a follow-up and we brought out the following day's sheet. On page four was a small, one-column spread. It was stated very simply. Herron Mallory, a small-time petty thief and former bootlegger, had been persuaded to drop the charges against Rudolph York. Apparently it was suspected that he couldn't make any headway against a solid citizen like York in the face of his previous convictions. That was where it ended. At least for the time being.

York had a damn good reason then to turn green when Mallory's name was mentioned. Pat tapped the clipping. "What do you think?"

"It might be the real McCoy . . . then again it might be an accident. I can't see why York would pull a stunt like that."

"There're possibilities here. York was no young man when his son was born. He might have wanted an heir awfully bad."

"I thought of that, Pat, but there's one strike

against it. If York was going to pull a switch, with his knowledge of genetics he certainly would have taken one with a more favorable family history, don't you think?"

"Yes, if he made the switch himself. But if it were left up to someone else . . . the nurse, for instance, the choice might have been pretty casual."

"But the nurse stated . . ."

"York was very wealthy, Mike."

"I get it. But there's another side too, Mallory, being a cheap chiseler, might have realized the possibilities in setting up a squawk after his own child died, and picked on York. Mallory would figure York would come across with some hard cash just to keep down that kind of publicity. How does that read?"

"Clever, Mike, very clever. But which one do you *believe?*"

The picture of York's face when he heard the name Mallory flashed across my mind. The terror, the stark terror; the hate. York the strong. He wouldn't budge an inch if Mallory had simply been trying some judicious blackmail. Instead, he would have been the one to bring the matter to the police. I said: "It was a switch, Pat."

"That puts it on Mallory."

I nodded. "He must have waited a long time for his chance. Waited until the kid was worth his weight in gold to York and the public, then put the snatch on him. Only he underestimated the kid and bungled the job. When York went

171

to Grange's place, Mallory followed him, thinking that York might have figured where the kidnapping came from and split his skull."

"Did you try to trace the cleaver, Mike?"

"No, it was the kind you could buy in any hardware store, and it was well handled, besides. A tool like that would be nearly impossible to trace. There was no sense in my fooling around with it. Price will track it down if it's possible. Frankly, I don't think it'll work. What's got me now is why someone ripped out this clipping in the Sidon library. Even as a stall it wouldn't mean much."

"It's bound to have a bearing."

"It'll come, it'll come. How about trying to run down Mallory for me? Think you can find anything on him?"

"We should, Mike. Let's go down to headquarters. If he was pinched at all we'll have a record of it."

"Roger." We were lucky enough to nab a cab waiting for the red light on the corner of Fifth and Forty-second. Pat gave him the downtown address and we leaned back into the cushions. Fifteen minutes later we got out in front of an old-fashioned red brick building and took the elevator to the third floor. I waited in an office until Pat returned bearing a folder under his arm. He cleared off the desk with a sweep of his hand and shook the contents out on the blotter.

The sheaf was fastened with a clip. The typewritten notation read, Herron Mallory. As dossiers go, it wasn't thick. The first page gave Mallory's history and record of his first booking. Age, 20 in 1927; born in New York City of Irish-Russian parents. Charged with operating a vehicle without a license. That was the starter. He came up on bootlegging, petty larceny; he was suspected of participating in a hijack-killing and a holdup. Plenty of charges, but a fine list of cases suspended and a terse "not convicted" written across the bottom of the page. Mr. Mallory either had a good lawyer or friends where it counted. The last page bore his picture, a profile and front view shot of a dark fellow slightly on the thin side with eyes and mouth carrying an inbred sneer.

I held it under the light to get a better look at it, studying it from every angle, but nothing clicked.

Pat said, "Well?"

"No good, chum. Either I never saw him before or the years have changed him a lot. I don't know the guy from Adam."

He held out a typewritten report. One that had never gotten past a police desk. I read it over. In short, it was the charges that Mallory had wanted filed against York for kidnapping his kid. No matter who Mallory was or had been, there was a note of sincerity in that statement. There was also a handwritten note on hospital stationery from Head Nurse Rita Cambell briefly decrying the charge as absolutely false. There was no doubt about it. Rita Cambell's note was aggressive and assuring enough to convince anyone that Mallory was all wet. Fine state of affairs. I had never participated in the mechanics of becoming a father, but I did know that the male parent was Johnny-the-Gom as far as the hospital was concerned. He saw his baby maybe once for two minutes through a tiny glass plate set in the door. Sure, it would be possible to recognize your child even in that time, but all babies do look alike in most ways. To the nurse actually in charge of the child's entire life, however, each one has the separate identity of a person. It was unlikely that she would make a mistake . . . unless paid for it. Damn, it *could* happen unless you knew nurses. Doubt again. Nurses had a code of ethics as rigid as a doctor's. Any woman who gave her life to the profession wasn't the type that would succumb to a show of long green.

Hell, I was getting all balled up. First I was sure it was a switch, now I wasn't so sure. Pat had seen the indecision in my face. He can figure things, too. "There it is, Mike. I can't do anything more because it's outside my jurisdiction, but if I can help you in any way, say the word."

"Thanks, kid. It really doesn't make much difference whether it was a switch or not. Someplace Mallory figures in it. Before I can go any further I'll have to find either Mallory or Grange, but don't ask me how. If Price turns up Grange I'll get a chance to talk to her, but if Dilwick is the one I'll be out in the cold."

Pat looked sour. "Dilwick ought to be in jail."

"Dilwick ought to be dead. He's a bastard."

"He's still the law, though, and you know what that means."

"Yeah."

Pat started stuffing the papers back in the folder, but I stopped him. "Let me take another look at them, will you?"

"Sure."

I rifled through them quickly, then shook my head.

"Something familiar?"

"No . . . I don't think so. There's something in there that's ringing a bell, but I can't put my finger on it. Oh, nuts, put 'em away."

We went downstairs together and shook hands in the doorway. Pat hailed a cab and I took the next one up to Fifty-fourth and Eighth, then out over to the parking lot. The day was far from being wasted; I was getting closer to the theme of the thing. On top of everything else there was a possible baby switch. It was looking up now. Here was an underlying motive that was as deep and unending as the ocean. The groping, the fumbling after ends that led nowhere was finished. This was meat that could be eaten. But first it had to be chewed; chewed and ground up fine before it could be swallowed.

My mind was hammering itself silly. The dossier. What was in the dossier? I saw something there, but what? I went over it carefully enough; I checked everything against everything else, but what did I forget?

The hell with it. I shoved the key in the ignition and stepped on the starter.

Chapter Nine

Going back to Sidon I held it down to a slow fifty, stopping only once for a quick bite and a tank of gas. Someday I was going to get me a decent meal. Someday. Three miles from the city I turned off the back road to a clover leaf, then swung onto the main artery. When I reached the state police headquarters I cut across the concrete and onto the gravel.

For once Price was in when I wanted him.

So was Dilwick.

I said hello to Price and barely nodded to Dilwick.

"You lousy slob!" he muttered softly.

"Shut up, pig."

"Maybe you both better shut up," Price put in quietly. I threw my hat on the desk and pushed a butt between my lips. Price waited until I lit it, then jerked his thumb toward the fat cop.

"He wants words with you, Mike."

"Let's hear 'em," I offered.

"Not here, wise guy. I think you'd do better at the station. I don't want to be interrupted."

That was a nasty dig at Price, and the sergeant took it right up. "Forget that stuff," he barked, "while he's here he's under my jurisdiction. Don't forget it."

For a minute I thought Dilwick was going to swing and I was hoping he would. I'd love to be in a two-way scramble over that guy. The odds were too great. He looked daggers at Price. "I won't forget it," he repeated.

Price led off. "Dilwick says you broke into the Grange apartment and confiscated something of importance. What about it, Mike?"

I let Dilwick have a lopsided grin. "Did I?"

"You know damn well you did! You'd better . . ."

"How do you know it was important?"

"It's gone, that's reason enough."

"Hell."

"Wait a minute, Mike," Price cut in. "What did you take?"

I saw him trying to keep his face straight. Price liked this game of baiting Dilwick.

"I could say nothing, pal, and he couldn't prove a thing. I bet you never found any prints of mine, did you, Dilwick?" The cop's face was getting redder. ". . . and the way you had that building bottled up nobody *should* have been able to get in, should they?" Dilwick would split his seams if I kept it up any longer. "Sure, I was there, so what? I found what a dozen of you missed."

I reached in my pocket and yanked out the two wills. Dilwick reached a shaking hand for them but I passed them to Price. "This old one was in Grange's apartment. It isn't good because this is the later one. Maybe it had better be filed some-place."

Dilwick was watching me closely. "Where did the second one come from?"

"Wouldn't you like to know?"

I was too slow. The back of Dilwick's hand nearly rocked my head off my shoulders. The arm of a chair hit my side and before I could spill over into it Dilwick had my shirt front. Price caught his hand before he could swing again.

I kicked the chair away and pulled free as Price stepped between us. "Let me go, Price!" I yelled.

"Damn it, I said to turn it off!"

Dilwick backed off reluctantly. "I'll play that back to you, Dilwick," I said. Nobody was pulling that trick on me and getting by with it. It's a won-der he had the nerve to start something after that last pasting I gave him. Maybe he was hoping I'd try to use my rod . . . that would be swell. He could knock me off as nice as anything and call it police business.

"Maybe you'll answer the next time you're spo-ken to, Hammer. You've pulled a lot of shady deals around here lately and I'm sick of it. As for you, Price, you're treating him like he's carrying a badge. You've got me hogtied, but that won't last long if I want to work on it."

The sergeant's voice was almost a whisper. "One day you're going to go too far. I think you know what I mean."

Evidently Dilwick did. His lips tightened into a thin line and his eyes blazed, but he shut up just the same. "Now if you have anything to say, say it properly."

With an obvious attempt at controlling his rage, Dilwick nodded. He turned to me again. "Where did you get the other will?"

"Wouldn't you like to know?" I repeated.

"You letting him get away with this, Price?"

The Trooper was on the spot. "Tell him, Mike."

"I'll tell you, Price. He can listen in. I found it among York's personal effects."

For a full ten minutes I stood by while the two of them went over the contents of the wills. Price was satisfied with a cursory examination, but not so Dilwick. He read every line, then reread them. I could see the muscles of his mouth twitch as he worked the thing out in his mind. No, I was not underestimating Dilwick one bit. There wasn't much that went on that he didn't know about. Twice, he let his eyes slide off the paper and meet mine. It was coming. Any minute now.

Then it was here. "I could read murder into this," he grated.

Price turned sharply. "Yes?"

"Hammer, I think I'm going to put you on the spot."

"Swell. You'd like that. Okay, go ahead."

"Pull up your ears and get a load of this, Price. This punk and the Nichols dame could make a nice team. Damn nice. You didn't think I'd find out about those pictures, did you, Hammer? Well, I did. You know what it looks like to me? It looks like the Nichols babe blackmailed Grange into

179

making York change his will. Let York see those shots and Grange's reputation would be shot to hell, she'd be fired and lose out on the will to boot. At least if she came through on the deal, all she'd lose was the will."

I nodded. "Pretty, but where do I come in?"

"Right now. Grange got hold of those pictures somehow. Only Nichols pulls a fast one and tells York that Grange was the one who was blackmailing her. York takes off for Grange's apartment in a rage because he had a yen for his pretty little niece, only Grange bumps him. Then Nichols corners you and you bump Grange and get the stuff off her, and the will. Now you turn it up, Nichols comes into a wad of cash and you split it."

It wasn't as bad as I thought. Dilwick had squeezed a lot of straight facts out of somebody, only he was putting it together wrong. Yeah, he had gotten around, all right. He had reached a lot of people to get that much and he'd like to make it stick.

Price said, "What about it, Mike?"

I grinned. "He's got a real sweet case there." I looked at the cop. "How're you going to prove it?"

"Never mind," he snarled. "I will, I will. Maybe I ought to book you right now on what I have. It'll hold up and Price knows it, too."

"Uh-uh. It'll hold up . . . for about five minutes. Did you find Grange yet?"

He said nothing.

"Nuts," I laughed, "no corpus delicti, no Mike Hammer."

"Wrong, Hammer. After a reasonable length of

time and sufficient evidence to substantiate death, a corpse can be assumed."

"He's right, Mike."

"Then he's got to shoot holes in my alibi, Price. I have a pretty tight one."

"Where did you go after you left Alice's apartment the other night?" Brother, I should have guessed it. Dilwick had put the bee on the Graham kid and the bastard copped a sneak. It was ten to one he told Dilwick he hadn't seen me.

That's what I get for making enemies. If the Graham kid thought he could put me on the spot he'd do it. So would Alice for that matter.

But there were still angles. "Go ahead and work on my alibi, Dilwick. You know what it is. Only I'll give you odds that I can make your witness see the light sooner than you can."

"Not if you're in the can."

"First get me there. I don't think you can. Even if you did a good lawyer could rip those phonies apart on the stand and you know it. You're stalling, Dilwick. What're you scared of? Me? Afraid I'll put a crimp in your doings?"

"You're asking for it, punk."

Price came back into the argument. "Skip it, Dilwick. If you have the goods on him then present it through the regular channels, only don't slip up. Let you and your gang go too far and there'll be trouble. I'm satisfied to let Mr. Hammer operate unhampered because I'm familiar with him . . . and you, too."

"Thanks, pal."

Dilwick jammed his hat on and stamped out of the room. If I wanted to get anywhere I was going to have to act fast, because my fat friend wasn't going to let any grass grow under his feet finding enough dope to toss me in the clink. When the door slammed I let Price have my biggest smile. He smiled right back.

"Where've you been?"

"New York. I tried to get you before I left but you weren't around."

"I know. We've had a dozen reports of Grange being seen and I've been running them down."

"Any luck?"

"Nothing. A lot of mistaken identities and a few cranks who wanted to see the police in action. What did you get?"

"Plenty. We're back to the kidnapping again. This whole pot of stew started there and is going to end there. Ruston wasn't York's kid at all. His died in childbirth and another was switched to take its place. The father of the baby was a small-time hoodlum and tried to make a complaint but was dissuaded along the line. All very nicely covered up, but I think it's a case of murder that's been brewing for fourteen years."

During the next half hour I gave him everything I knew, starting with my trip to the local library. Price was a lot like Pat. He sat there saying nothing, taking it all in and letting it digest in his mind. Occasionally he would nod, but never interrupted until I had finished.

182

He said: "That throws the ball to this Mallory character."

"Roger, and the guy is completely unknown. The last time he showed up was a few days after the switch took place."

"A man can change a lot in fourteen years."

"That's what I'm thinking," I agreed. "The first thing we have to do is concentrate on locating Grange. Alive or dead she can bring us further up to date. She didn't disappear for nothing."

"All right, Mike, I'll do my share. I still have men dragging the channel and on the dragnet. What are you going to do?"

"There are a few members of the loyal York clan that I'd like to see. In the meantime do you think you can keep Dilwick off my neck?"

"I'll try, but I can't promise much. Unfortunately, the law is made up of words which have to be abided more by the letter than the spirit therein, so to speak. If I can sidetrack him I will, but you had better keep him under observation if you can. I don't have to tell you what he's up to. He's a stinker."

"Twice over. Okay. I'll keep in touch with you. Thanks for the boost. The way things are I'm going to have to be sharp on my end to beat Dilwick out of putting me up at the expense of the city."

Dusk had settled around the countryside like a gray blanket when I left headquarters. I stepped into the car and rolled out the drive to the highway. I turned toward the full glow that marked the lights of Sidon and pulled into the town at suppertime.

I would have gone straight to the estate if I hadn't passed the library which was still lit up.

It was just an idea, but I've had them before and they'd paid off. I slammed the brakes on, backed up and parked in front of the building. Inside the door I noticed the girl at the desk, but she wasn't the same one I had spoken to before. This one had legs like a bridge lamp. Thinking that perhaps Legs was in one of the reading rooms, I toured the place, but aside from an elderly gentleman, two schoolteacher types and some kids, the place was empty.

Just to be sure I checked the cellar, too, but the light was off and I didn't think she'd be down there in the dark even if Grange was with her. Not with that musty-tomb odor anyway.

The girl at the desk said, "Can I help you find something, sir?"

"Maybe you can."

"What book was it?"

I tried to look puzzled. "That is what I forgot. The girl that was here this morning had it all picked out for me. Now I can't find her."

"Oh, you mean Miss Cook?"

"Yeah," I faked, "that's the one. Is she around now?"

This time the girl was the one to be puzzled. "No, she isn't. She went home for lunch this afternoon and never returned. I came on duty early to replace her. We've tried to locate her all over town, but she seems to have dropped from sight. It's so very strange."

It was getting hot now, hotter than ever. The little bells were going off inside my skull. Little bells that tinkled and rang and chimed and beat themselves into shattered pieces of nothing. It was getting hotter, this broth, and I was holding onto the handle.

"This Miss Cook. Where does she live?"

"Why, two blocks down on Snyder Avenue. Shall I call her apartment again? Perhaps she's home now."

I didn't think she'd have any luck, but I said, "Please do."

She lifted the receiver and dialed a number. I heard the buzz of the bell on the other end, then the voice of the landlady answering. No, Miss Cook hadn't come in yet. Yes, she would tell her to call as soon as she did. Yes. Yes. Good night.

"She isn't there."

"So I gathered. Oh, well, she's probably had one of her boy friends drop in on her. I'll come back tomorrow."

"Very well, I'm sorry I couldn't help you."

Sorry, everybody was being sorry. Pretty soon somebody was going to be so sorry they died of it. Snyder Avenue was a quiet residential section of old brownstone houses that had undergone many a face-lifting and emerged looking the same as ever. On one corner a tiny grocery store was squeezed in between buildings. The stout man in the dirty white apron was taking in some boxes of vegetables as he prepared to close up shop. I drew abreast of him and whistled.

When he stopped I asked, "Know a Miss Cook? She's the librarian. I forgot which house it was."

"Yeah, sure." He pointed down the block. "See that car sitting under the streetlight? Well the house just past it and on the other side is the one. Old Mrs. Baxter is the landlady and she don't like noise, so you better not honk for her."

I yelled my thanks and went up the street and parked behind the car he had indicated. Except for the light in the first floor front, the place was in darkness. I ran up the steps and looked over the doorbell. Mrs. Baxter's name was there, along with four others, but only one bell.

I pushed it.

She must have been waiting for me to make up my mind, because she came out like a jack-in-the-box.

"Well?"

"Mrs. Baxter?"

"That's me."

"I'm looking for Miss Cook. They . . ."

"Who ain't been looking for her. All day long the phone's been driving me crazy, first one fellow then another. When she gets back here I'm going to give her a good piece of my mind."

"May I come in, Mrs. Baxter?"

"What for? She isn't home. If she didn't leave all her things here I'd say she skipped out. Heaven only knows why."

I couldn't stand there and argue with her. My wallet slipped into my palm and I let her see the glint of the metal. Badges are wonderful things

186

even when they don't mean a thing. Her eyes went from my hand to my face before she moistened her lips nervously and stood aside in the doorway.

"Has . . . has there been trouble?"

"We don't know." I shut the door and followed her into the living room. "What time did she leave here today?"

"Right after lunch. About a quarter to one."

"Does she always eat at home?"

"Only her lunch. She brings in things and . . . you know. At night she goes out with her boy friends for supper."

"Did you see her go?"

"Yes. Well, no. I didn't see her, but I heard her upstairs and heard her come down. The way she always takes the stairs two at a time in those high heels I couldn't very well not hear her."

"I see. Do you mind if I take a look at her room? There's a chance that she might be involved in a case we're working on and we don't want anything to happen to her."

"Do you think . . ."

"Your guess is as good as mine, Mrs. Baxter. Where's her room?"

"Next floor in the rear. She never locks her door so you can go right in."

I nodded and went up the stairs with the old lady's eyes boring holes in my back. She was right about the door. It swung in when I turned the knob. I shut the door behind me and switched on the light, standing there in the middle of the room for a minute taking it all in. Just a room, a nice, neat girl's room. Everything was in its place, nothing was disarranged. The closet was well stocked with clothes including a fairly decent mink coat inside a plastic bag. The drawers in the dresser were the same way. Tidy. Nothing gone.

Son of a bitch, *she* was snatched too! I slammed the drawer shut so hard a row of bottles went over. Why didn't I pick her up sooner. She was Myra Grange's alibi! Of course! And somebody was fighting pretty hard to keep Myra Grange's face in the mud. She didn't skip out on her own . . . not and leave all her clothes here. She went out that front door on her way back to work and she was picked up somewhere between here and the library. Fine, swell. I'd made a monkey of myself by letting things slide just a little longer. I wasn't the only one who knew that she and Grange were on more than just speaking terms. That somebody was either following me around or getting there on his own hook.

A small desk and chair occupied one corner of the room beside the bed. A small letter-writing affair with a flap front was on the desk. I pulled the cover down and glanced at the papers neatly placed in the pigeonholes. Bills, receipted bills. A few notes and some letters. In the middle of the blotter a writing tablet looked at me with a blank stare.

The first three letters were from a sailor out of town. Very factual letters quite unlike a sailor. Evidently a relative. Or a sap. The next letter was the payoff. I breezed through it and felt the sweat pop out on my face. Paragraph after paragraph of lurid, torrid love . . . words of endearment . . . more love, exotic, fantastic.

Grange had signed only her initials at the bottom.

When I slid the letter back I whistled through my teeth. Grange had certainly gone whole hog with her little partner. I would have closed the desk up after rifling through the rest of the stuff if I hadn't felt that squeegy feeling crawling around my neck. It wasn't new. I had had it in Pat's office.

Something I was supposed to remember. Something I was supposed to see. Damn. I went back through the stuff, but as far as I could see there wasn't anything there that I had seen before I came into the room. Or was there?

Roger . . . there was! It was in my hand. I was staring at Grange's bold signature. It was the handwriting that I had recognized. The first time I had seen it was on some of her papers I had taken from that little cache in her apartment. The next time I had seen it was on the bottom of a statement certifying that Ruston was York's son and not Mallory's, only that time the signature read *Rita Cambell*.

It hit me like a pile driver, hard, crushing. It had been dangling in front of my face all this time and I hadn't seen it. But I wasn't alone with the knowledge, hell no. Somebody else had it too, that's why Grange was dead or missing and Cook on the lam.

Motive, at last the motive. I stood alone in the

middle of the room and spun the thing around in my mind. This was raw, bitter motive. It was motive that incited kidnapping and caused murder and this was proof of it. The switch, the payoff. York taking Grange under his wing to keep the thing quiet. Crime that touched off crime that touched off more crime like a string of firecrackers. When you put money into it the thing got bigger and more scrambled than ever.

I had gotten to the center of it. The nucleus. Right on the target were Ruston and Grange. Somebody was aiming at both of them. Winged the kid and got Grange. Mallory, but who the hell was he? Just a figure known to have existed, and without doubt still existing.

I needed bait to catch this fish, yet I couldn't use the kid; he had seen too much already. That is, unless he was willing. I felt like a heel to put it up to him. But it was that or try to track Grange down. Senseless? I didn't know. Maybe a dozen cops *had* dragged the river, and maybe the dragnet *was* all over the state, but maybe they were going at it the wrong way. Sure, maybe it would be best to try for Grange. She was bound to have the story if anyone had, and I wouldn't be taking a chance with the kid's neck either.

Mrs. Baxter was waiting for me at the foot of the stairs, wringing her hands like a nervous hen. "Find anything?" she asked.

I nodded. "Evidence that she expected to come back here. She didn't just run off."

"Oh, dear."

190

"If anyone calls, try to get their names, and keep a record of all calls. Either Sergeant Price of the state police will check on it or me personally. Under no conditions give out the information to anyone else, understand?"

She muttered her assent and nodded. I didn't want Dilwick to pull another fasty on me. As soon as I left, all the lights on the lower floor blazed on. Mrs. Baxter was the scary type, I guess.

I swung my heap around in a U-turn, then got on the main street and stopped outside a drugstore. My dime got me police headquarters and headquarters reached Price on the radio. We had a brief chitchat through the medium of the desk cop and I told him to meet me at the post in fifteen minutes.

Price beat me there by ten feet and came over to see what was up.

"You have the pictures of Grange's car after it went in the drink?"

"Yeah, inside, want to see them?"

"Yes."

On the way in I told him what had happened. The first thing he did was go to the radio and put out a call on the Cook girl. I supplied the information the best I could, but my description centered mainly about her legs. They were things you couldn't miss. For a few minutes Price disappeared into the back room and I heard him fiddling around with a filing cabinet.

He came out with a dozen good shots of the wrecked sedan. "If you don't mind, tell me what

191

you're going to do with these?"

"Beats me," I answered. "It's just a jumping-off place. Since she's still among the missing she can still be found. This is where she was last seen apparently."

"There've been a lot of men looking for her."

I grinned at him. "Now there's going to be another." Each one of the shots I went over in detail, trying to pick out the spot where it went in, and visualizing just how it turned in the air to land like it did. Price watched me closely, trying to see what I was getting at.

"Price . . ."

"Yes."

"When you pulled the car out, was the door on the right open?"

"It was, but the seat had come loose and was jammed in the doorway. She would have had some time trying to climb out that way."

"The other door was open too?"

His head bobbed. "The lock had snapped when the door was wrenched open, probably by the force of hitting the water, although being on the left, it could have happened when her car was forced off the road."

"Think she might have gotten out that way?"

"Gotten out . . . or floated out?"

"Either one."

"More like it was the other way."

"Was the car scratched up much?"

The sergeant looked thoughtful. "Not as much as it should have been. The side was punched in from the water, and the front fender partially crumpled where it hit the bottom, but the only new marks were short ones along the bottom of the door and on the very edge of the fender, and at that we can't be sure that they didn't come from the riverbed."

"I get it," I said. "You think that she was scared off the road. I've seen enough women drivers to believe that, even if she was only half a dame. Why not? Another car threatening to slam into her would be reason enough to make her jump the curb. Well, it's enough for me. If she was dead there wouldn't be much sense keeping her body hidden, and if it weren't hidden it would have shown up by now, so I'm assuming that Grange is still alive somewhere and if she's alive she can be found."

I tossed the sheaf of pictures back to Price. "Thanks, chum. No reflection on any of you, but I think you've been looking for Grange the wrong way. You've been looking for a body."

He smiled a bit and we said good night. What had to be done had to wait until morning . . . the first thing in the morning. I tooled my car back to town and called the estate. Harvey was glad to hear from me, yes, everything was all right. Billy had been in the yard with Ruston all day and Miss Malcom had stayed in her room. The doctor had been there again and there was nothing to worry about. Ruston had been asking for me. I told Harvey to tell the kid I'd drop up as soon as I could and not to worry. My last instructions still went. Be sure the place was locked up tight, and that Billy stayed near the kid and Roxy. One thing I did make sure of. Harvey was to tell the gatekeeper what was in the bottle that he thought contained aspirin.

When I hung up I picked up another pack of butts, a clean set of underwear, shirt and socks in a dry goods store, then threw the stuff in the back of the car and drove out around town until I came to the bay. Under the light of the half-moon it was black and shimmering, an oily, snaky tongue that searched the edges of the shore with frightened, whimpering sounds. The shadows were black as pitch, not a soul was on the streets. Three-quarters of a mile down the road one lone window winked with a yellow, baleful eye.

I took advantage of the swath Grange had cut in the restraining wire and pulled up almost to the brink of the drop-off, changed my mind, pulled out and backed in, just in case I had to get out of there in a hurry. When I figured I was well set I opened my fresh deck of butts, chain-smoked four of them in utter silence, then closed up the windows to within an inch of the top, pulled my hat down over my eyes and went to sleep.

The sun was fighting back the night when I woke up. Outside the steamed-up windows a gray fog was drifting up from the waters, coiling and uncoiling until the tendrils blended into a low-hanging blanket of haze that hung four feet over the ground.

It looked cold. It was cold. I was going to be kicking myself a long time if nothing came of this. I stripped off my clothes throwing them into the car until I was standing shivering in my underwear. Well, it was one way to get a bath, anyway. I could think of better ways.

A quick plunge. It had to be quick or I would change my mind. I swam out to the spot I had fixed in my mind; the spot where Grange's car had landed. Then I stopped swimming. I let myself go as limp as possible, treading water just enough to keep my head above the surface. You got it. I was supposed to be playing dead, or almost dead. Half knocked out maybe. The tide was the same, I had checked on that. If this had been just another river it wouldn't have mattered, but this part was more an inlet than anything else. It emptied and filled with the tides, having its own peculiarities and eddies. It swirled and washed around objects long sunk in the cove of the bottom. I could feel it tug at my feet, trying to drag me down with little monkey hands, gentle, tugging hands that would mean nothing to a swimmer, but could have a noticeable effect on someone half dazed.

Just a few minutes had passed and I was already out of sight of the car around the bend. Here the shores drew away as the riverbed widened until it reached the mouth of the inlet opening into the bay. I thought that I was going to keep right on drifting by, and had about made up my mind to quit all this damn foolishness when I felt the first effect of the eddy.

It was pulling me toward the north shore. A little thrill of excitement shot through me, and although I was numb I felt an emotional warmth dart into my bones. The shore was closer now. I began to spin in a slow, tight circle as something underneath me kicked up a fuss with the water. In another moment I saw what was causing the drag. A tiny U-bend in the shoreline jutted out far enough to cause a suction in the main flow and create enough disturbance to pull in anything not too far out.

Closer . . . closer . . . I reached out and got hold of some finger-thick reeds and held on, then steadied myself with one hand in the mud and clambered up on the shore. There were no tracks save mine, but then again there wouldn't be. Behind me the muck was already filling in the holes my feet had made. I parted the reeds, picking my way through the remains of shellfish and stubble. They were tough reeds, all right. When I let them go they snapped back in place like a whip. If anyone had come out of the river it would have been here. It *had* to be here!

The reeds changed into scrub trees and thorny brush that clawed at my skin, raking me with their needlepoints. I used a stick as a club and beat at them, trying to hold my temper down. When they continued to eat their way into my flesh I cursed them up and down.

But the next second I took it all back. They were nice briars. Beautiful briars. The loveliest briars I had ever seen, because one of them was sporting part of a woman's dress.

I could have kissed that torn piece of fabric. It was stained, but fresh. And nobody was going to go through those reeds and briars except the little sweetheart I was after. This time I was gentler with the bushes and crawled through them as best I could without getting myself torn apart. Then the brush gave way to grass. That green stuff felt better than a Persian rug under my sore feet. I sat down on the edge of the clearing and picked the thorns out of my skin.

Then I stood up and shoved the tail end of my T-shirt down into my shorts. Straight ahead of me was a shack. If ever there was an ideal hiding place, this was it, and as long as I was going to visit its occupant I might as well look my charming best.

I knocked, then kicked the door open. A rat scurried along the edge of the wall and shot past my feet into the light. The place was as empty as a tomb. But it *had* been occupied. Someone had turned the one room into a shambles. A box seat was freshly splintered into sharp fragments on the floor, and the makeshift stove in the middle of the room lay on its side. Over in the corner a bottle lay smashed in a million pieces, throwing jagged glints of light to the walls. She had been here. There was no doubt of it. Two more pieces of the same fabric I held in my hand were caught on the frayed end of the wooden table. She had put up a hell of a fight, all right, but it didn't do her any good.

When the voice behind me said, "Hey, you!"

197

I pivoted on my heel and my hand clawed for the gun I didn't have. A little old guy in baggy pants was peering at me through the one lens of his glasses, wiping his nose on a dirty hunk of rag at the same time.

"That's not healthy, Pop."

"You one of them there college kids?" he asked.

I eased him out the door and came out beside him. "No, why?"

"Always you college kids what go around in yer shorts. Seed some uptown once." He raised his glasses and took a good look at my face; "Say . . . you ain't no college kid."

"Didn't say I was."

"Well, what you guys joining? I seed ya swimming in the crick, just like the other one."

I went after that *other one* like a bird after a bug. "What other one?" My hands were shaking like mad. It was all I could do to keep my hands off his shirt and shake the facts out of him.

"The one what come up t'other day. Maybe it was yesterday. I disremember days. What ya joining?"

"Er . . . a club. We have to swim the river then reach the house without being seen. Guess they won't let me join now that somebody saw me. Did you see the other guy too?"

"Sure. I seed him, but I don't say nothing. I seed lotta funny things go on and I don't ask no questions. It's just that this was kinda funny, that's all."

"What did he look like?"

"Well, I couldn't see him too good. He was big and fat. I heered him puffing plenty after he come out of the weeds. Yeah, he was a big feller. I didn't know who he was so I went back through the woods to my boat."

"Just the other guy, that's all you saw?"

"Yep."

"Nobody else?"

"Nope."

"Anybody live in that shack?"

"Not now. Comes next month and Pee Wee'll move in. He's a tramp. Don't do nothing but fish and live like a pig. He's been living there three summers now."

"This other one you saw, did he have a mean-looking face, sort of scowling?"

"Ummmm. Now that you mention it, he looked kinda mad. Guess that was one reason why I left."

Dilwick. It was Dilwick. The fat slob had gotten the jump on me again. I knew he was smart . . . he had to be to get along the way he did, but I didn't think he was that smart. Dilwick had put the puzzle together and come out on top. Dilwick had found Grange in the shack and carted her off. Then why the hell didn't he produce her? Maybe the rest of the case stunk, but this part raised a putrid odor to high heaven. Everybody under the sun wanted in on the act, now it was Dilwick. Crime upon crime upon crime upon crime. Wasn't it ever going to end? Okay, fat boy, start playing games with me. You think you pulled a quickie, don't you? You think nobody knows about this

. . . T.S., junior, I know about it now, and brother, I think I'm beginning to see where I'm going.

"How can I get back to the bridge without swimming, Pop?"

He pointed a gnarled finger toward the tree line. "A path runs through there. Keeps right along the bank, but stick to it and nobody'll see ya in ya jeans. Hope they let ya join that club."

"I think I can fix it." I batted away the bugs that were beginning to swarm around me and took off for the path. Damn Dilwick anyway.

Chapter Ten

Going back was rough. My feet were bleeding at the end of the first hundred yards and the blue-tailed flies were making my back a bas-relief of red lumps. Some good samaritan had left a dirty burlap bag that reeked of fish and glinted with dried scales in the path and I ripped it in half and wrapped the pieces over my instep and around my ankles. It wasn't so bad after that.

By the time I reached the bridge the sun was hanging well up in the sky and a few office workers were rolling along the road on their way to town. I waited until the road was clear, then made a dash across the bridge to the car and climbed into some dry clothes. My feet were so sore I could hardly get into my shoes, but leaving the laces open helped a little. I threw the wet shorts in the back with the rest of the junk and reached for a butt. There are times when a guy wants a cigarette in the worst way, and this was one of them.

I finished two, threw the car in gear and plowed out to the concrete. Now the fun began. Me and Dilwick were going to be as inseparable as clamshells. Grange was the key to unlock this mess. Only Dilwick had Grange. Just to be certain I pulled into a dog wagon and went to the pay phone. Sergeant Price was in again. It was getting to be a habit.

I said hello, then: "Get a report on Grange yet, Sergeant?"

He replied in the negative.

"How about the city cops?"

"Nothing there either. I thought you were looking for her?"

"Yeah . . . I am. Look, do me a favor. Buzz the city bulls and see if they've turned up anything in the last few hours. I'll hold on."

"But they would have called me if . . ."

"Go on, try it anyway."

Price picked up another phone and dialed. I heard him ask the cop on the desk the question, then he slammed the receiver down. "Not a thing, Mike."

"Okay, that's all I want to know." I grinned to myself. It was more than a feud between the city and the state police; it was monkey business. But it was all right with me. In fact, I was happier about it than I should have been. I was looking forward to kicking Dilwick's teeth right down his big fat yap.

But before I did anything I was going to get some breakfast. I went through my first order, had seconds, then went for another round. By that time the counterman was looking at the stubble of the beard on my face and wondering whether or not I was a half-starved tramp filling my belly then going to ask to work out the check.

When I threw him a ten his eyes rolled a little. If he didn't check the serial number of that bill to see if it was stolen I didn't know people. I collected my change and glanced at the time. Ten-fifteen. Dilwick would be getting to his office about now. Swell.

This time I found a spot on the corner and pulled in behind a pickup truck. I shut off the motor then buried my nose in a magazine with one eye on the station house across the street. Dilwick came waddling up five minutes later. He disappeared inside and didn't show his face for two hours. When he did come out he was with one of the boys that had worked over Billy that night.

The pair stepped into an official car and drove down the street, turning onto Main. I was two cars behind. A half mile down they stopped, got out and went into a saloon. I took up a position where I could cover the entrance.

That was the way the day went; from one joint to another. By five o'clock I was dying for a short beer and a sandwich, and the two decided to call it quits. Dilwick dumped his partner off in front of a modern, two-story brick building, then cut across town, beating out a red light on the way. By the time I had caught up with him he was locking the car up in front of a trim duplex. He never saw me, not because I slouched down in my seat as I shot by, but because he was waving to a blonde in the window.

I only got a glimpse of her well-rounded shoulders and ample bust, but the look on her face told me that I had might as well go home because this was going to be an all-night affair.

No sense taking any chances. I bought a container of coffee and some sandwiches in a delicatessen then circled the block until I eased into the curb across the street and fifty yards behind the police buggy. The sandwiches went in a hurry. On top of the dash I laid out my cigs and a pack of matches, then worked the seat around until I was comfortable. At nine o'clock the lights went out in the duplex. Twenty cigarettes later they were still out. I curled up on the seat and conked off.

I was getting to hate the morning. My back ached from the swim yesterday and the cramped position behind the wheel. I opened the door and stretched my legs, getting a peek at myself in the rear-vision mirror. I didn't look pretty. Dilwick's car was still in front of the duplex.

"Have a rough night?"

I raised my eyebrows at the milkman. He was grinning like a fool.

"See a lot of you guys around this morning. Want a bottle of milk? It's good and cold."

"Hell yeah, hand one over." I fished in my pocket and threw him a half.

"Someday," he said, "I'm going to sell sandwiches on this route. I'll make a million."

He walked off whistling as I yanked the stopper out and raised the bottle to my lips. It was the best drink I ever had. Just as I reached the bottom the door opened in the duplex. A face peered around, then Dilwick walked out hurriedly. I threw the empty bottle to the grass beside the curb then waited until the black sedan had turned the corner before I left my position. When I reached the intersection Dilwick was two blocks ahead. Tailing him was too easy. There were no cars out that early to screen me. When he stopped at a diner I kept right on going to the station house and got my old spot back, hoping that I hadn't made a mistake in figuring that Dilwick would come back to his castle after he had breakfast.

This time I was lucky. He drove up a half hour later.

Forcing myself to be patient was brutal. For four solid hours Dilwick went through the saloon routine solo, then he picked up his previous companion. At two in the afternoon he acquired another rummy and the circus continued. I was never far behind. Twice, I hopped out and followed them on foot, then scrambled for my heap when they came out of a joint. Six o'clock they stopped in a chop suey joint for supper and I found a chance to get a shave and watch them at the same time from a spot on the other side of the avenue. If this kept up I'd blow my top. What the hell was Dilwick doing with Grange anyway? What goes on in a town where all the cops do is tour the bars and spend their nights shacking up with blondes? If Grange was such a hot potato why wasn't Dilwick working on her? Or did he have her stashed away somewhere . . . or what could be worse, maybe I was all wet in thinking Dilwick had her in the first place.

Nuts.

I had a coffee and was two cigarettes to the good when the trio came out of the restaurant, only this time they split up in front of the door, shaking hands all around. Dilwick got in the car, changed his mind and walked down to a liquor store. When he came out with a wrapped bottle under his arm the other two were gone. Good, this was better. He slid under the wheel and pulled out. I let a convertible get between us and went after him. No blonde tonight. Dilwick went through town taking his time until he reached the highway, stopped at one of those last chance places for a beer while I watched from the spacious driveway, unwrapped his bottle before he started again and had a swig.

By the time he was on the highway it was getting dark. What a day. Five miles out of Sidon he turned right on a black macadam road that wound around the fringes of some good-sized estates and snapped on his lights. I left mine off. Wherever he was going, he wasn't in a hurry. Apparently the road went nowhere, twisting around hills and cutting a swath through the oaks lining the roads. After a while the estates petered out and the countryside, what was visible of it, became a little wild.

Ahead of me his taillight was a red eye, one that paced itself at an even thirty-five. On either side of me were walls of Stygian blackness, and

I was having all I could do to stay on the road. I had to drive with one eye on the taillight and the other on the macadam, but Dilwick was making it easy for me by taking it slow.

Too easy. I was so busy driving I didn't see the other car slide up behind me until it was too late. They had their lights out too.

I hit the brakes as they cut across my nose, my hand fumbling for my rod. Even before I stopped the guy had leaped out of the car and was reaching through my window for me. I batted the hand away from my neck then got slammed across my eyes with a gun barrel. The door flew open. I kicked out with my feet and somebody grunted. Somehow I got the gun in my hand, but another gun lashed out of the darkness and smashed across my wrist.

Damn, I was stupid! I got mousetrapped! Somehow I kicked free of the car and swung. A formless shape in front of me cursed and grunted. Then a light hit me full in the face. I kicked it out of a hand, but the damage had been done. I couldn't see at all. A fist caught me high on the head as a pair of arms slipped around my waist and threw me into a fender. With all my strength I jerked my head back and caught the guy's nose. The bone splintered and hot blood gushed down my collar.

It was kick and gouge and try to get your teeth in something. The only sounds were of fists on flesh and feet on the road. Heavy breathing. I broke free for a moment, ducked, and came in punching. I doubled one up when I planted my knuckles in his belly up to the wrist. A billy swooshed in the air, missed and swooshed again. I thought my shoulder was broken. I got so damn mad I let somebody have it in the shins and he screamed in pain when I nearly busted the bone with my toe. The billy caught me in the bad shoulder again and I hit the ground, stumbling over the guy who was holding his leg. He let go long enough to try for my throat, but I brought my knee up and dug it in his groin.

All three of us were on the ground, rolling in the dirt. I felt cold steel under my hand and wrapped my fingers around a gun butt as a foot nearly ripped me in half. The guy with the billy sent one tearing into my side that took the breath out of my lungs. He tried again as I rolled and grazed me, then landed full on my gut with both his knees. Outlined against the sky I could see him straddling me, the billy raised in the air, ready to crush in my skull. Little balls of fire were popping in my brain and my breath was still a tight knot in my belly when that shot-weighted billy started to come down.

I raised the gun and shot him square in the face, blowing his brains all over the road.

But the billy was too much to stop. It was pulled off course yet it managed to knock me half-senseless when it grazed my temple. Before I went completely out I heard feet pounding on the road and an engine start up. The other guy wasn't taking any chances. He was clearing out.

I lay there under a corpse for three-quarters of

an hour before I had enough strength to crawl away. On my hands and knees I reached my car and pulled myself erect. My breath came in hot, jerky gasps. I had to bend to one side to breathe at all. My face felt like a truck went over it and I was sticky with blood and guts, but I couldn't tell how much of it was my own. From the dash I pulled a flashlight and played its beam over the body in the road. Unless he had some identifying scars, nobody would ever be able to tell who he was. Ten feet away from his feet his brainpan lay like a gooey ashtray on the road.

His pockets held over a hundred bucks in cash, a wallet with a Sidon police shield pinned to it and a greasy deck of cards. The billy was still in his hand. I found my own gun, cleaned off the one I had used and tossed it into the bushes. It didn't matter whether they found it or not. I was going to be number-one client in a murder case.

Lousy? It was stinking. I was supposed to have been rubbed out. All very legal, of course. I was suspiciously tailing a cop down a dark road with my lights out, and when ordered to halt put up a fight and during it got myself killed. Except it didn't happen that way. I nailed one and the other got away to tell about it. Maybe Dilwick would like it better this way.

So they caught me. They knew I was trailing them all day and laid a lot of elaborate plans to catch me in the trap. I had to get out of there before that other one got back with reinforcements. I let the body stay as it was, then crawled under the wheel and drove onto the grass, swinging around the corpse, then back on the highway. This time I used my lights and the gas pedal, hightailing it away as fast as I could hold the turns. Whenever I reached an intersection I cut off on it, hoping it wasn't a dead end. It took me a good two hours to circle the town and come out in the general vicinity of York's place, but I couldn't afford using the highway.

The car was in my way now; it could be spotted too easily. If they saw me it would be shoot to kill and I didn't have the kind of artillery necessary to fight a gang war. Dilwick would have every cop in town on the lookout, reporting the incident to Price only after they cornered me somewhere and punched me full of holes, or the death of the cop was printed in the papers.

There was only one reason for all the hoodah . . . Grange was still the key, and Dilwick knew I knew he had her.

Trusting luck that I wasn't too far from home, I ran the car off the road between the trees, pulling as far into the bushes as I could get. Using some cut branches for camouflage I covered up the hood and any part that could be seen by casual observation from the road. When I was satisfied I stepped out and began walking in a northerly direction.

A road finally crossed the one I was on with phone wires paralleling it. A lead from a pole a hundred yards down left the main line and went into the trees. When I reached it I saw the sleepy little bungalow hidden in the shadows. If my feet on the pavement didn't wake the occupants, my sharp rapping did.

Inside someone said, "George . . . the door."

Bedsprings creaked and the guy mumbled something then crossed the room to the door. A light went on overhead and when the guy in the faded bathrobe took a look at me he almost choked.

"I had an accident. Do you have a phone?"

"Accident? Yeah . . . yeah. Come in."

He gulped and glancing at me nervously, called, "Mary. It's a man who's had an accident. Anything I can do for you, mister? Anybody else hurt?"

The guy back there would never feel anything again. "No, nobody else is hurt."

"Here's the phone." His wife came out while I dialed Price's number. She tried to fuss around with a wet rag, wiping the blood off my face, but I waved her off. Price wasn't there, but I got his home number. He wasn't there either, he had left for headquarters. The woman was too excited. I insisted that I didn't need a doctor, but let her go over my battered face with the rag, then dialed headquarters again.

Price was there. He nearly exploded when he heard my voice. "What the hell happened? Where are you?"

"Out of town. What are you doing up at this hour?"

"Are you kidding? A police reporter slipped me the news that a cop was killed south of town. I got the rest from Dilwick. You're in a jam now."

"You're not telling me anything new," I said. "Has he got the police combing the town for me?"

"Everyone on the force is out. I had to put you on the Teletype myself. All the roads are blocked and they have a cordon around York's house. Are you giving yourself up?"

"Don't be silly. I'd be sticking my head in a noose. As far as Dilwick is concerned I have to be knocked off. It's a screw pitch, pal, and I'm in it deep, but don't believe all you hear."

"You killed him, didn't you?"

"You're damn right. If I hadn't it would have been me lying back there with my head in sections all over the ground. They squeezed me good. I was tailing Dilwick, but they got wise and tailed me. Like a damn fool I let Dilwick lead me out in the sticks and they jumped me. What was I supposed to do, take it lying down? They didn't have orders to pick me up, they were supposed to knock me off."

"Where are you? I'll come out and get you."

"No dice, buddy, I have work to do."

"You'd better give yourself up, Mike. You'll be safer in the custody of the law."

"Like hell. Dilwick will have me held under his jurisdiction and that's what he wants. He'll be able to finish the job then."

"Just the same, Mike . . ."

"Say, whose side are you on?"

He didn't say a word for a full minute. "I'm a policeman, Mike. I'll have to take you in."

He was making it hard for me. "Listen, don't

be a sap, Price, something's come up that I have to follow."

"What?"

I glanced at the two faces that were taking in every word. "I can't tell you now."

"The police can handle it."

"In a pig's eye. Now listen. If you want to see this case solved you'll have to stay off my back as much as you can. I know something that only the killer knows and I have to use it while it's hot. If you take me in it'll be too late for both of us. You know what Dilwick and his outfit are like. So I shot one of them. That's hardly killing a cop, is it? Then don't get so upset about me blasting a cheap crook. Do you want to see this case wrapped up or not?"

"Of course."

"Then keep your boys out of this. I'm not worried about the rest."

There was another silent period while he thought it over, then he spoke. "Mike, I shouldn't do this; it's against all rules and regulations. But I know how things stand and I still want to be a good cop. Sometimes to do that you have to fall in line. I'll stay off you. I don't know how long it will be before the pressure gets put on me, but until then I'll do what I can."

"Thanks, pal. I won't run out on you."

"I know that."

"Expect to hear from me every once in a while. Just keep the calls under your hat. If I need you I'll yell for help."

"I'll be around, Mike. You'd better steer clear of York's place. That place is alive with city cops."

"Roger . . . and thanks again."

When I cradled the phone I could see a thousand questions getting ready to come my way. The guy and his wife were all eyes and ears and couldn't make sense out of my conversation. It had to be a good lie to be believed.

I shoved my badge under their noses. "You've overheard an official phone conversation," I said brusquely. "Under no circumstances repeat any part of it. A band of thieves has been operating in this neighborhood under the guise of being policemen and we almost got them. Unfortunately one got away. There's been difficulty getting co-operation from the local police, and we have been operating under cover. In case they show up here you saw nothing, heard nothing. Understand?"

Wide-eyed, their heads bobbed in unison and I let myself out through the door. If they believed that one they were crazy.

As soon as I was in the shadows I turned up the road toward York's estate. Cops or no cops I had to get in there someway. From the top of a knoll I looked down the surrounding countryside. In the distance the lights of Sidon threw a glow into the sky, and here and there other lights twinkled as invisible trees flickered between us in the night breeze. But the one I was interested in was the house a bare mile off that was ablaze with lights in every window and ringed with the twin beams of headlights from the cars patroling the grounds. Occasionally one would throw a spotlight into the bushes, a bright finger of light trying to pin down a furtive figure. Me.

The hell with them. This was one time I couldn't afford a run-in with the bulls. I cut across the fields until the dark shape of a barn loomed ahead. Behind it was a haystack. It was either one or the other. I chose the stack and crawled in. It would take longer for the cows to eat me out than it would for some up-with-the-sun farmer to spot me shacking up with bossy. Three feet into the hay I shoved an armload of the stuff into the tunnel I had made, kicked my feet around until I had a fair-sized cave and went to sleep.

The sun rose, hit its midpoint then went down before I moved. My belly was rumbling with hunger and my tongue was parched from breathing chaff. If a million ants were inside my shirt I couldn't have felt more uncomfortable. Keeping the stack between me and the house, I crawled through the grass to the watering trough and brushed away the dirt that had settled on top of the water. If I thought that last bottle of milk was the best drink I ever had, I was wrong. When I could hold no more I splashed my face and neck, letting it soak my shirt, grinning with pleasure.

I heard the back door of the house slam and took a flying dive to the other side of the trough. Footsteps came closer, heavy, boot-shod feet. When I was getting set to make a jump I noticed that the steps were going right on by. My breath came a little easier. Sticking my head out from behind the trough I saw the broad back of my host disappearing into the barn. He was carrying a pail in either hand. That could mean he was coming over to the trough. I had it right then. Trying to step softly, I ducked into a crouch and made a dash for the darkness of the tree line.

Once there I stripped to the skin and dusted myself off with my shirt. Much better. A bath and something to eat and I would feel almost human. Sometime during the night my watch had stopped and I could only guess at the time. I put it at an arbitrary nine-thirty and wound it up. Still too early. I had one cigarette left, the mashed, battered remains of a smoke. Shielding the match I fired it up and dragged it down to my fingernails. For two hours I sat on a stump watching a scud of clouds blot out the stars and feeling little crawling things climb up my pants leg.

The bugs were too much. I'd as soon run the risk of bumping into a cordon of Dilwick's thugs. When my watch said ten after eleven I skirted the edge of the farm and got back on the road. If anyone came along I'd see them a mile away. I found my knoll again. The lights were still on in York's house, but not in force like they had been. Only one pair of headlights peered balefully around the grounds.

An hour later I stood opposite the east wall leaning over the edge of a five-foot drainage ditch with my watch in my hands. At regular six-minute intervals the outlines of a man in a slouch hat and raincoat would drift past. When he reached the end of the wall he turned and came back. There were two of them on this side. Always, when they met at the middle of the wall, there would be some smart retort that I couldn't catch. But their pacing was regular. Dilwick should have been in the Army. A regular beat like that was a cinch to sneak through. Once a car drove by checking up on the men and tossing a spot into the bushes, but from that angle the ditch itself was completely concealed by the foot-high weeds that grew along its lip.

It had to be quick. And noiseless.

It took the guy three minutes to reach the end of the wall, three minutes to get back to me again. Maybe three-quarters of a minute if he ran. When he passed the next time I checked my watch, keeping my eyes on the second hand. One, two, two and a half. I gripped the edge of the ditch. Ten seconds, five . . . I crouched . . . now! Vaulting the ditch I ducked across the road to the wall. Ten feet away, the tree I had chosen waved to me with leafy fingers. I jumped, grabbed the lowest limb and swung up, then picked my way up until I was even with the wall. My clothes caught on spikelike branches, ripped loose, then caught again.

Feet were swishing. Feet that had a copper over them. This was the second phase. If he looked up and saw me outlined against the sky I was sunk. I palmed the .45 and threw the safety off, waiting. They came closer. I heard him singing a tuneless song under his breath, swearing at briars that bit at his ankles.

He was under the tree now, in the shadows. The singing stopped. The feet stopped. My hand tightened around the butt of the gun, aiming it where his head would be. If he saw me he was held in his tracks. I would have let one go at him if I didn't see the flare of the match in time. When his butt was lit he breathed the smoke in deeply then continued on his rounds. I shoved the gun back and put the watch on him again until it read another three minutes.

Button your coat . . . be sure nothing was going to jingle in your pockets . . . keep your watch face blacked out . . . hold tight . . . get ready . . . and jump. For one brief moment I was airborne before my fingers felt the cold stone wall. The corner caught me in the chest and I almost fell. Somehow I kicked my feet to the top and felt broken glass cemented in the surface shatter under my heels. Whether or not anybody was under me, I had to jump, I was too much of a target there on the wall. Keeping low I stepped over the glass and dropped off.

I landed in soft turf with hardly a sound, doubled up and rolled into a thorny rosebush. The house was right in front of me now; I could pick out Roxy's window. The pane was still shattered from the bullet that had pierced it and nicked her.

Ruston's window was lit, too, but the shade was drawn. Behind the house the police car stopped, some loud talking ensued, then it went forward again. No chance to check schedules now. I had to hope that I wasn't seen. Just as soon as the car passed I ran for the wall of the building, keeping in whatever cover the bushes and hedgerows afforded. It wasn't much, but I made the house without an alarm going off. The wrist-thick vine that ran up the side wasn't as good as a ladder, but it served the purpose. I went up it like a monkey until I was just below Roxy's window.

I reached up for the sill, grabbed it and as I did the damn brick pulled loose and tumbled down past me landing with a raucous clatter in the bushes below and then bounced sickeningly into other bricks with a noise as loud as thunder in my ears. I froze against the wall, heard somebody call out, then saw a bright shaft of light leap out from a spot in someone's hand below and watched it probe the area where the brick had landed.

Whoever he was didn't look up, not expecting anyone above him. His stupidity was making me feel a little better and I figured I had it made. I wasn't that lucky. There was too much weight on the vine and I felt it beginning to pull loose from wherever it was anchored in the wall above my head.

I didn't bother trying to be careful. Down below a couple of voices were going back and forth and their own sounds covered mine. I scrambled up, reached and got hold of an awning hook imbedded in the concrete of the exterior frame of the window and hung on with one hand, my knee reaching for the sill before I could pull the hook out of the wall.

Down below everybody was suddenly satisfied

and the lights went out. In the darkness I heard feet taking up the vigil again. I waited a full minute, tried the window, realized that it was locked then tapped on the pane. I did it again, not a frantic tapping, but a gentle signaling that got a response I could hear right through the glass. I hoped she wouldn't scream, but would think it out long enough to look first.

She did.

There was enough reflected light from a bed lamp to highlight my face and I heard her gasp, reach for the latch and ease the window up. I rolled over the sill, dropped to the floor and let her shut the window behind me and pull down the blind. Only then did she snap on the light.

"Mike!"

"Quiet, kid, they're all over the place downstairs."

"Yes, I know." Her eyes filled up suddenly and she half-ran to me, her arms folding me to her.

Behind us there was a startled little gasp. I swung, pushed Roxy away from me, then grinned. Ruston was standing there in his pajamas, his face a dead white. "Mike!" he started to say, then swayed against the doorjamb. I walked over, grabbed him and rubbed his head until he started to smile at me.

"You take it easy, little buddy . . . you've had it rough. How about letting me be the only casualty around here. By the way, where is Billy?"

Roxy answered. "Dilwick took him downstairs and is making him stay there."

"Did he get rough with him?"

"No . . . Billy said he'd better lay off or he'd get a lawyer that would take care of that fat goon and Dilwick didn't touch him. For once Billy stood up for himself."

Ruston was shaking under my hand. His eyes would dart from the door to the window and he'd listen attentively to the heavy footsteps wandering down in the rooms below. "Mike, why did you come? I don't want them to see you. I don't care what you did, but you can't let them get you."

"I came to see you, kid."

"Me?"

"Uh-huh."

"Why?"

"I have something big to ask you."

The two of them stared at me, wondering what could be so great as to bring me through that army of cops. Roxy, quizzically; Ruston with his eyes filled with awe. "What is it, Mike?"

"You're pretty smart, kid, try to understand this. Something has come up, something that I didn't expect. How would you like to point out the killer for me? Be a target. Lead the killer to you so I can get him?"

"Mike, you can't!"

I looked at Roxy. "Why not?"

"It isn't fair. You can't ask him to do that!"

I slumped in a chair and rubbed my head. "Maybe you're right. It is a lot to expect."

Ruston was tugging at my sleeve. "I'll do it, Mike. I'm not afraid."

I didn't know what to say. If I missed I'd never be able to look at myself in the face again, yet here was the kid, ready and trusting me not to miss. Roxy sank to the edge of the bed, her face pale, waiting for my answer. But I couldn't let a killer run around loose.

"Okay, Lancelot, it's a deal." Roxy was hating me with her eyes. "Before we go over it, do you think you can get me something to eat?"

"Sure, Mike. I'll get it. The policemen won't bother me." Ruston smiled and left. I heard him going down the stairs, then tell the cop he was hungry and so was his governess. The cop growled and let him go.

Roxy said, "You're a louse, Mike, but I guess it has to be that way. We almost lost Ruston once, and it's liable to happen again if somebody doesn't think of something. Well, you did. I just hope it works, that's all."

"So do I, kid."

Ruston came running up the stairs and slipped into the room, bearing a pair of enormous sandwiches. I all but snatched them out of his hand and tore into them wolfishly. Once, the cop came upstairs and prowled past the door and I almost choked. After he went by, the two of them laughed silently at me standing there with my rod in my hand and the remains of a sandwich sticking out of my mouth.

Roxy went over and pressed her ear to the door, then slowly turned the key in the lock. "I suppose you'll leave the same way you came in, Mike, so maybe that'll give you more time if you have to go quickly."

"Gee, I hope nothing happens to you, Mike. I'm not afraid for myself, I'm just afraid what those policemen will do. They say you shot a cop and now you have to die."

"Lancelot, you worry too much."

"But even if you find out who's been causing all the trouble the police will still be looking for you, won't they?"

"Perhaps not," I laughed. "They're going to be pretty fed up with me when I bust this case."

The kid shuddered, his eyes closed tightly for a second. "I keep thinking of that night in the shack. The night you shot one of those men that kidnapped me. It was an awful fight."

I felt as though a mule had kicked me in the stomach. "What did you say?"

"That night . . . you remember. When you shot that man and . . ."

I cut him off. "You can get off that target, Ruston," I said softly. "I won't need you for a decoy after all."

Roxy twisted toward me, watching the expression in my eyes. "Why, Mike?"

"I just remembered that I shot a guy, that's why. I had forgotten all about it." I jammed on my hat and picked up a pack of Roxy's butts from the dresser. "You two stay here and keep the door locked. I can get the killer, now, by damn, and I won't have to make him come to me either. Roxy, turn that light off. Give me five minutes after I leave before you turn it on again. Forget you ever saw me up here or Dilwick will have your scalp."

The urgency in my voice moved her to action. Without a word in reply she reached out for the light and snapped it off. Ruston gasped and moved toward the door, with the slightest tremor of excitement creeping into his breathing. I saw him silhouetted there for an instant, a floor lamp right in front of him. Before I could caution him the shade struck him in the face. His hand went out . . . hit the lamp and it toppled to the floor with the popping of the bulb and the crash of a fallen tree. Or so it seemed.

Downstairs a gruff voice barked out. Before it could call again I threw the window up and went out, groping for the vine. Someplace in the house a whistle shrilled and angry fists beat at the door. Half-sliding, half-climbing, I went down the side of the building. Another whistle and somebody got nervous and let a shot blast into the confusion. From every side came the shouts and the whistles. Just before I reached the ground a car raced up and two figures leaped out. But I was lucky. The racket was all centered on the inside of the house and the coppers were taking it for granted that I was trapped there.

As fast as I could go, I beat it across the drive to the lawn, then into the trees. Now I knew where I was. One tree ahead formed the perfect ladder over the wall. I had my gun out now in case that patrol was waiting. There would be no command to halt, just a volley of shots until one of us dropped. All right, I was ready. Behind me a window smashed and Roxy screamed. Then there was a loud "There he goes!" and a pair of pistols spit fire. With the trees in the way and the distance opening between us, I wasn't concerned about getting hit.

The tree was a godsend. I went up its inclined trunk thanking whatever lightning bolt had split it in such a handy fashion, made the top of the wall and jumped for the grass. The sentries weren't there anymore. Probably trying to be in on the kill.

A siren screamed inside the wall and the chase was on, but it would be a futile chase now. Once in the tree line on the other side of the road I took it easy. They'd be looking for a car and the search would be along the road. So long, suckers!

Chapter Eleven

I slept in my car all night. It wasn't until noon that I was ready to roll. Now the streets would be packed with traffic and my buggy would be just another vehicle. There were hundreds like it on the road. Superficially it was a five-year-old heap that had seen plenty of service, but the souped-up motor under the hood came out of a limousine that had packed a lot of speed and power. Once on the road nothing the city cops had was going to catch me.

Good old Ruston. If my memory had been working right I wouldn't have forgotten my little pal I plugged. Guys who are shot need doctors, and need them quick, and in Sidon there wouldn't be that many medics that I couldn't run them all down. A crooked doc, that's what I wanted. If a gunshot had been treated Price would have known about it and told me, but none had been entered in the books. Either a crooked doc or a threatened doc. He was the one to find.

I stripped the branches from the fenders and cleared a path to the road, and then eased out onto the macadam. At the first crossroad a sign pointed to the highway and I took the turn. Two

226

miles down I turned into a stream of traffic, picked out a guy going along at a medium clip and nosed in behind him.

We both turned off into the city, only I parked on a side street and went into a candy store that had a public phone. Fiddling through the Yellow Pages, I ripped out the sheet of doctors listed there, and went through the motions of making a phone call. Nobody bothered to so much as glance at me.

Back in the car I laid out my course and drove to the first on my list. It wasn't an impressive list. Seven names. Dr. Griffin was stepping out of his car when I pulled in.

"Doctor . . ."

"Yes?"

His eyes went up and down the ruin of my suit. "Don't mind me," I said. "I've been out all night chasing down the dick that shot that cop. I'm a reporter."

"Oh, yes, I heard about that. What can I do for you?"

"The police fired several shots at him. There's a chance that he might have been hit. Have you treated any gunshot wounds lately?"

He drew himself up in indignant pride. "Certainly not! I would have reported it immediately had I done so."

"Thank you, Doctor."

The next one wasn't home, but his housekeeper was. Yes, she knew all about the doctor's affairs. No, there had been no gunshot wounds since Mr.

Dillon shot himself in the foot like a silly fool when loading his shotgun. Yes, she was very glad to be of service.

Dr. Pierce ushered me into his very modern office personally. I pulled the same reporter routine on him. "A gunshot wound, you say?"

"Yes. It wasn't likely that he'd treat it himself."

He folded his hands across his paunch and leaned back in his chair. "There was one the day before yesterday, but I reported that. Certainly you know about it. A .22-caliber bullet. The man was hit while driving out in the country. Said he didn't know where it came from."

I covered up quickly. "Oh, that one. No, this would have been a larger shell. The cops don't pack .22's these days."

"I expect not," he laughed.

"Well, thanks anyway, Doctor."

"Don't mention it."

Four names left. It was past three o'clock. The next two weren't home, but the wife of one assured me that her husband would not have treated any wounds of the sort because he had been on a case in the hospital during the entire week.

The other one was in Florida on a vacation.

Dr. Clark had offices a block away from police headquarters, a very unhealthy place right now. Cars drove up and away in a constant procession, but I had to chance it. I parked pointing away from the area, making sure I had plenty of room to pull out, my wheels turned away from the curb. A woman came out of the office holding a baby.

Then a man walking on a cane. I didn't want to enter an office full of people if I could help it, but if he didn't get rid of his patients in a hurry I was going to have to bust in anyway. A boy went in crying, holding his arm. Damn it, I was losing time!

As I went to reach for the ignition switch another guy came out, a four-inch wide bandage going from the corner of his mouth to his ear. The bells again. They went off all at once inside my skull until I wanted to scream. The bandage. The hell with the gunshot wound, he was probably dead. The bandage. My fingers hooking in a mouth and ripping the skin wide open. Of course, he'd need a doctor too! You wouldn't find two freak accidents like that happening at once. He was a ratty-looking guy dressed in a sharp gray suit with eyes that were everywhere at once. He went down the steps easily and walked to a car a couple ahead of me. I felt my heart beginning to pound, beating like a heavy hammer, an incredible excitement that made my blood race in my veins like a river about to flood.

He pulled out and I was right behind him, our bumpers almost touching. There was no subtlety about this tail job, maybe that's why I got away with it so long. He didn't notice me until we were on the back road six miles out of town ripping off seventy miles an hour. Just the two of us. We had left all other traffic miles behind. I saw his eyes go to the rear-vision mirror and his car spurted ahead. I grinned evilly to myself and stepped down harder on the accelerator until I was pushing him again.

His eyes hardly left the mirror. There was fright in them now. A hand went out and he signaled me to pass. I ignored it. Eighty-five now. A four-store town went by with the wind. I barely heard the whistle of the town cop blast as I passed him. Eighty-seven. The other car was having trouble holding the turns. It leaned until the tires screamed as the driver jerked it around. I grinned again. The frame of my car was rigged for just such emergencies. Ninety. Trees shot by like a huge picket fence. Another town. A rapid parade of identical billboards advertising a casino in Brocton. Ninety-five. A straightaway came up lined with more billboards. A nice flat stretch was ahead, he would have opened up on it if he could have, but his load was doing all it could. At the end of the straightaway was the outline of a town.

My little friend, you have had it, I said to myself. I went down on the gas, the car leaped ahead, we rubbed fenders. For a split second I was looking into those eyes and remembering that night, before I cut across his hood. He took to the shoulder, fought the wheel furiously but couldn't control it. The back end skidded around and the car went over on its side like a pinwheel. I stood on the brake, but his car was still rolling as I stopped.

I backed up and got out without shutting the engine off. The punk was lucky, damn lucky. His car had rolled but never up-ended, and those steel turret top jobs could take it on a roll in soft earth.

He was crawling out of the door reaching under his coat for a rod when I jumped him. When I slapped him across that bandage he screamed and dropped the gun. I straddled him and picked it up, a snub-nosed .38, and thrust it in my waistband.

"Hello, pal," I said.

Little bubbles of pink foam oozed from the corners of his mouth. "Don't . . . don't do nothing . . ."

"Shut up."

"Please . . ."

"Shut up." I looked at him, looked at him good. If my face said anything he could read it. "Remember me? Remember that night in the shack? Remember the kid?"

Recognition dawned on him. A terrible, fearful recognition and he shuddered the entire length of his body. "What're ya gonna do?"

I brought my hand down across his face as hard as I could. He moaned and whimpered, "Don't!" Blood started to seep through the bandage, bright red now.

"Where's the guy I shot?"

He breathed, "Dead," through a mouthful of gore. It ran out his mouth and dribbled down his chin.

"Who's Mallory?"

He closed his eyes and shook his head. All right, don't talk. Make me make you. This would be fun. I worked my nails under the adhesive of the bandage and ripped it off with one tug. Clotted

231

blood pulled at his skin and he screamed again. A huge half-open tear went from the corner of his mouth up his jawline, giving him a perpetual grin like a clown.

"Open your eyes." He forced his lids up, his chest heaved for air. Twitches of pain gripped his face. "Now listen to me, chum. I asked you who Mallory was. I'm going to put my fingers in your mouth and rip out those stitches one by one until you tell me. Then I'm going to open you up on the other side. If you'd sooner look like a clam, don't talk."

"No! I . . . I don't know no Mallory."

I slapped him across the cheek, then did as I promised. More blood welled out of the cut. He screamed once more, a short scream of intolerable agony. "Who's Mallory?"

"Honest . . . don't know . . ."

Another stitch went. He passed out cold.

I could wait. He came to groaning senselessly. I shook his head until his eyes opened. "Who do you work for, pal?"

His lips moved, but no sound came forth. I nudged him again. "The boss . . . Nelson . . . at the casino."

Nelson. I hadn't heard it before. "Who's Mallory?"

"No more. I don't know . . ." His voice faded out to nothing and his eyes shut. Except for the steady flow of blood seeping down his chin he looked as dead as they come.

It was getting dark again. I hadn't noticed the cars driving up until the lights of one shone on me. People were piling out of the first car and running across the field, shouting at each other and pointing to the overturned car.

The first one was all out of breath when he reached me. "What happened, mister? Is he dead? God, look at his face!"

"He'll be all right," I told him. "He just passed out." By that time the others were crowded around. One guy broke through the ring and flipped his coat open to show a badge.

"Better get him to a hospital. Ain't none here. Nearest one's in Sidon." He yanked a pad out of his pocket and wet the tip of a pencil with his tongue. "What's your name, mister?"

I almost blurted it out without thinking. If he heard it I'd be under his gun in a second, and there wasn't much I could do with this mob around. I stood up and motioned him away from the crowd. On the other side of the upturned car I looked him square in the eye.

"This wasn't an accident," I said, "I ran him off the road."

"You what?"

"Keep quiet and listen. This guy is a kidnapper. He may be a killer. I want you to get to the nearest phone and call Sergeant Price of the state police, understand? His headquarters is on the highway outside of Sidon. If you can't get him, keep trying until you do."

His hands gripped my lapels. "Say, buster, what are you trying to pull? Who the hell are you, any-way?"

"My name is Mike . . . Mike Hammer. I'm wanted by every crooked cop in this part of the state and if you don't get your paws off me I'll break your arm!"

His jaw sagged, but he let go my coat, then his brows wrinkled. "I'll be damned," he said. "I always did want to meet you. Read all the New York papers y' know. By damn. Say, you *did* kill that Sidon cop, didn't you?"

"Yes, I did."

"By damn, that's good. He put a bullet into one of our local lads one night when he was driving back from the casino. Shot him while he was dead drunk because he didn't like his looks. He got away with it too, by damn. What was that you wanted me to tell the police?"

I breathed a lot easier. I never thought I'd find a friend this far out. "You call Price and tell him to get out to the casino as fast as his car will bring him. And tell him to take along some boys."

"Gonna be trouble?"

"There's liable to be."

"Maybe I should go." He pulled at his chin, thinking hard. "I don't know. The casino is all we got around here. It ain't doing us no good, but the guy that runs it runs the town."

"Stay out of it if you can help it. Get an ambulance if you want to for that guy back there, but forget the hospital. Stick him in the cooler. Then get on the phone and call Price."

"Okay, Mike. I'll do that for you. Didn't think you shot that cop in cold blood like the notices

234

said. You didn't, did you?"

"He was sitting on top of me about to bash my brains out with a billy when I shot the top of his head off."

"A good thing, by damn."

I didn't hang around. Twenty pairs of eyes followed me across the field to my car, but if there was any explaining to be done the cop was making a good job of it. Before I climbed under the wheel he had hands helping to right the car and six people carrying the figure of The Face to the road.

Nelson, the Boss. Another character. Where did he come in? He wasn't on the level if rat-puss was working for him. Nelson, but no Mallory. I stepped on the starter and ran the engine up. Nelson, but no Mallory. Something cold rolled down my temple and I wiped it away. Sweat. Hell, it couldn't be true, not what I was thinking, but it made sense! Oh, hell, it was impossible, people just aren't made that way! The pieces didn't have to be fitted into place any longer . . . they were being drawn into a pattern of murder as if by a magnet under the board, a pattern of death as complicated as a Persian tapestry, ugly enough to hang in Hitler's own parlor. Nelson, but no Mallory. The rest would be only incidental, a necessary incidental. I sweated so freely that my shirt was matted to my body.

I didn't have to look for the killer any longer. I knew who the killer was now.

The early crowd had arrived at the casino in

235

force. Dozens of cars with plates from three states were already falling into neat rows at the direction of the attendant and their occupants in evening dress and rich business clothes were making their way across the lawn to the doors. It was an imposing place built like an old colonial mansion with twenty-foot pillars circling the entire house. From inside came the strains of a decent orchestra and a lot of loud talk from the bar on the west side. Floodlights played about the grounds, lighting up the trees in the back and glancing off the waters of the bay with sparkling fingers. The outlines of a boathouse made a dark blot in the trees, and out in the channel the lights from some moored yachts danced with the roll of the ships.

For five minutes I sat in the car with a butt hanging between my lips, taking in every part of the joint. When I had the layout pretty well in my mind I stepped out and flipped the attendant a buck. The guy's watery eyes went up and down my clothes, wondering what the hell I was doing there.

"Where'll I find Nelson, friend?"

He didn't like my tone, but he didn't argue about it. "What do you want him for?"

"We got a load of special stuff coming in on a truck and I want to find out what he wants done with it."

"Booze?"

"Yeah."

"Hell, ain't he taking the stuff off Carmen?"

"This is something special, but I'm not jawing

about it out here. Where is he?"

"If he ain't on the floor he'll be upstairs in his office."

I nodded and angled over to the door. Two boys in shabby tuxedos stood on either side throwing greetings to the customers. They didn't throw any to me. I saw them exchange glances when they both caught the outlines of the rod under my coat. One started drifting toward me and I muttered, "I got a truckload of stuff for the boss. When it comes up get it around the back. We had a police escort all the way out of Jersey until we lost them."

The pair gave me blank stares wondering what I was talking about, but when I brushed by them they fingered me an okay thinking I was on the in. Bar noises came from my left, noises you couldn't mistake. They were the same from the crummiest joint in the Bronx to the swankiest supper club uptown. I went in, grabbed a spot at the end and ordered a brew. The punk gave me a five-ounce glass and soaked me six bits for it. When he passed me my change I asked for the boss.

"Just went upstairs a minute ago." I downed the drink and threaded my way out again. In what had been the main living room at one time were the bobbing heads of the dancers, keeping time to the orchestra on the raised dais at one end. Dozens of white-coated waiters scurried about like ants getting ready for winter, carrying trays loaded to the rims with every size glass there was. A serving bar took up one whole end of the corridor with three bartenders passing out drinks. This place was a gold mine.

I went up the plush-carpeted stairs with traffic. It was mostly male. Big fat guys chewing on three-buck cigars carrying dough in their jeans. An occasional dame with a fortune in jewelry dangling from her extremities. At the top of the landing the whir of the wheels and the click of the dice came clearly over the subdued babble of tense voices seated around the tables. Such a beautiful setup. It would be a shame to spoil it. So this was what Price had referred to. Protected gambling. Even with a hundred-way split to stay covered the boss was getting a million-dollar income.

The crowd went into the game rooms, but I continued down the dimly lit hallway past the rest rooms until I reached another staircase. This one was smaller, less bright, but just as plush and just as well used. Upstairs someone had a spasm of coughing and water splashed in a cooler.

I looked around me, pressing flat against the wall, then ducked around the corner and stood on the first step. The gun was in my hand, fitting into its accustomed spot. One by one I went up the stairs, softly, very softly. At the top, light from a doorway set into the wall threw a yellow light on the paneling opposite it. Three steps from the landing I felt the board drop a fraction of an inch under my foot. That was what I was waiting for.

I hit the door, threw it open and jammed the rod in the face of the monkey in the tux who was about to throw the bolt. "You should have done that sooner," I sneered at him.

He tried to bluff it out. "What the hell do you think you're doing?"

"Shut up and lay down on the floor. Over here away from the door."

I guess he knew what would happen if he didn't. His face went white right down into his collar and he fell to his knees then stretched out on the floor like he was told. Before he buried his map in the nap of the carpet he threw me one of those "you'll-be-sorry" looks.

Like hell I'd be sorry. I wasn't born yesterday. I turned the gun around in my hand and got behind the door. I didn't have long to wait. The knob turned, a gun poked in with a guy behind it looking for a target, a leer of pure sadistic pleasure on his face. When I brought the butt of the .45 across his head the leer turned to amazement as he spilled forward like a sack of wet cement. The skin on his bald dome was split a good three inches from the thong hook on the handle and pulled apart like a gaping mouth. He would be a long time in sleepy town.

"You ought to get that trip fixed in the stairs," I said to the fancy boy on the floor. "It drops like a trapdoor."

He looked back at me through eyes that seemed to pulse every time his heart beat. Both his hands were on the floor, palms down, his body rising and falling with his labored breathing. Under a trim moustache his chin fell away a little, quivering like the rest of him. A hairline

239

that had once swept across his forehead now lay like low tide on the back of his head, graying a little, but not much. There was a scar on one lip and his nose had been twisted out of shape not too long ago, but when you looked hard you could still see through the wear of the years.

He was just what I expected. "Hello, Mallory," I said, "or should I say, Nelson?"

I could hardly hear his voice. "W . . . who are you?"

"Don't play games, sucker. My name is Mike Hammer. You ought to know me. I bumped one of your boys and made a mess of the other awhile back. You should see him now. I caught up with him again. Get up."

"What . . . are you going . . . to do?" I looked down at the .45. The safety was off and it was the nastiest-looking weapon in existence at that moment. I pointed it at his belly.

"Maybe I'll shoot you. There." I indicated his navel with the muzzle.

"If it's money you want, I can give it to you, Hammer. Please, get the rod off me."

Mallory was the tough guy. He edged away from me, holding his hands out in a futile attempt to stop a bullet if it should come. He stopped backing when he hit the edge of the desk. "I don't want any of your dough, Mallory," I said, "I want you." I let him look into the barrel again. "I want to hear something you have to say."

"I . . ."

"Where's Miss Grange . . . or should I say Rita Cambell?"

He drew his breath in a great swallow and before I could move swung around, grabbed the pen set from the desk and sent the solid onyx base crashing into my face.

Fingers clawed at my throat and we hit the floor with a tangle of arms and legs. I brought my knee up and missed, then swung with the gun. It landed on the side of his neck and gave me a chance to clear my head. I saw where the next punch was going. I brought it up from the floor and smacked him as hard as I could in the mouth. My knuckles pushed back his lips and his front teeth popped like hollow things under the blow.

The bastard spit them right in my face.

He was trying to reach my eyes. I tossed the rod to one side and laughed long and loud. Only for that one moment did he possess any strength at all, just that once when he was raging mad. I got hold of both his arms and pinned them down, then threw him sideways to the floor. His feet kicked out and kicked again until I got behind him. With his back on the floor I straddled his chest and sat on his stomach, both his hands flat against his sides, held there by my legs. He couldn't yell without choking on his own blood and he knew it, but he kept trying to spit at me nevertheless.

With my open palm I cracked him across the cheek. Right, left, right, left. His head went sideways with each slap, but my other hand always straightened it up again. I hit him until the palms of my hands were sore and his cheek split in a dozen places from my ring. At first he flopped and moaned for me to stop, then fought bitterly to get away from the blows that were tearing his face to shreds. When he was almost out, I quit.

"Where's Grange, Mallory?"

"The shed." He tried to plead with me not to hit him, but I cracked him one anyway.

"Where's the Cook girl?"

No answer. I reached for my rod and cradled it in my hand.

"Look at me, Mallory."

His eyes opened halfway. "My hand hurts. Answer me or I use this on you. Maybe you won't live through it. Where's the Cook girl?"

"Nobody else. Grange . . . is the . . . only one."

"You're lying, Mallory."

"No . . . just Grange."

I couldn't doubt but what he was telling the truth. After what I gave him he was ready to spill his guts. But that still didn't account for Cook. "Okay, who does have her then?" Blood bubbled out of his mouth from his split gums. "Don't know her."

"She was Grange's alibi, Mallory. She was with the Cook dame the night York was butchered. She would have given Grange an out."

His eyes came open all the way. "She's a bitch," he mouthed. "She doesn't deserve an alibi. They kidnapped my kid, that's what they did!"

"And you kidnapped him back . . . fourteen years later."

242

"He was mine, wasn't he? He didn't belong to York."

I gave it to him slowly. "You didn't really want him, did you? You didn't give a damn about the kid. All you wanted was to get even with York. Wasn't that it?"

Mallory turned his head to one side. "Answer me, damn you!"

"Yes."

"Who killed York?"

I waited for his answer. I had to be sure I was right. This was one time I had to be sure.

"It . . . it wasn't me."

I raised the gun and laid the barrel against his forehead. Mallory was staring into the mouth of hell. "Lie to me, Mallory," I said, "and I'll shoot you in the belly, then shoot you again a little higher. Not where you'll die quick, but where you'll wish you did. Say it was you and you die fast . . . like you don't deserve. Say it wasn't you and I may believe you and I may not . . . only don't lie to me because I know who killed York."

Once more his eyes met mine, showing pain and terror. "It . . . wasn't me. No, it wasn't me. You've got to believe that." I let the gun stay where it was, right against his forehead. "I didn't even know he was dead. It was Grange I wanted."

Even with his shattered mouth the words were coming freely as he begged for his life. "I got the news clipping in the mail. The one about the trouble in the hospital. There was no signature, but the letter said that Grange was Rita Cambell and she was a big shot now and if I kidnapped the kid, instead of ransom I could get positive information from York that his kid was my son. I wouldn't have snatched him if it wasn't so easy. The letter said the watchman on the gate would be drugged and the door to the house open on a certain night. All I had to do to get the kid was go in after him. I was still pretty mad at York and the letter made it worse. I wanted Myra Grange more than the old man, that's why when those crazy lugs I sent after the kid lost him I made a try for her. I followed her from her house to another place then waited for her to come out before I grabbed her. She was in there when York was killed and I was waiting outside. Honest, I didn't kill him. She didn't know who I was until I told her. Ever since that time when York stole my kid I used the name Nelson. She started to fight with me in the car and hit me over the head with the heel of her shoes. While I was still dizzy she beat it and got in her car and scrammed. I chased her and forced her off the road by the river and she went in. I thought she was dead. . . ."

The footsteps coming up the stairs stopped him. I whipped around and sent a shot crashing through the door. Somebody swore and yelled for reinforcements. I prodded Mallory with the tip of the rod. "The window and be quick."

He didn't need any urging. The gun in his back was good incentive. That damn warning trip. Either it went off someplace else or the boys on the doors got suspicious. Egghead was starting to groan on the floor. "Get the window up."

Mallory opened the catch and pushed. Outside the steel railings of the fire escape were waiting. I thanked the good fathers who passed the law making them compulsory for all three-story buildings. We went out together, then down the metal stairs without trying to conceal our steps. If I had a cowbell around my neck I couldn't have made more noise. Mallory kept spitting blood over the side, trying to keep his eyes on me and the steps at the same time. Above us heavy bodies were ramming the door. The lock splintered and some one tripped over the mug on the floor, but before they could get to the window we were on the ground.

"The boathouse. Shake it, Mallory, they won't care who they hit," I said.

Mallory was panting heavily, but he knew there was wisdom in my words. A shot snapped out that was drowned in a sudden blast from the orchestra, but I saw the gravel kick up almost at my feet. We skirted the edge of cars and out in between the fenders, then picked an opening and went through it to the boathouse. The back of it was padlocked.

"Open it."

"I . . . I don't have the key."

"That's a quick way to get yourself killed," I reminded him.

He fumbled for a key in his pocket, brought it out and inserted it in the padlock. His hands were shaking so hard that he couldn't get it off the hasp. I shoved him away and ripped it loose myself. The door slid sideways, and I thumbed him in, closing the door behind us. With the gun in the small of his back I flicked a match with my fingernail.

Grange and Cook were lying side by side in a pile of dirt at the far end of the boathouse. Both were tied up like Thanksgiving turkeys with a wad of cloth clamped between their jaws. They were out cold. Mallory's mouth dropped to his chin and he pointed a trembling finger at Cook. "She's here!"

"What the hell did you expect?"

His face grew livid until blood flowed afresh from his mouth. Mallory might have said something in anger if the match had not scorched my finger. I dropped it and cursed. He pulled away from the gun at the same time and ran for it. I took four steps toward the door, my arms outstretched to grab him, but he wasn't there. At the other end of the room one of the girls started to moan through her gag. A knob turned and for a second I saw stars in the sky at the side of the wall. My first shot got him in the leg and he fell to the floor screaming. In the half-light of the match I hadn't seen that side door, but he knew it was there. I ran over and yanked him back by the foot, mad enough to send a bullet into his gut.

I never had the chance. There was a blast of gunfire and my rod was torn from my grasp. The beam of a spotlight hit me in the eyes as Dilwick's voice said, "Freeze, Hammer. You make one move and I'll shoot hell out of you."

The light moved over to the side, never leaving me. Dilwick snapped on the overhead; one dim bulb that barely threw enough light to reach both ends. He was standing there beside the switch with as foul a look as I ever hope to see on a human face and murder in his hands. He was going to kill me.

It might have ended then if Mallory hadn't said, "You lousy rat. You stinking, lousy rat. You're the one who's been bleeding me. You son of a bitch."

Dilwick grinned at me, showing his teeth. "He's a wise guy, Hammer. Listen to him bawl."

I didn't say a word.

Dilwick went over and got my gun from the floor, using his handkerchief on the butt, never taking his eyes from either of us. He looked at me, then Mallory, and before either of us could move sent a shot smashing into Mallory's chest from my .45. The guy folded over in a quarter-roll and was still. Dilwick tossed the still-smoking gun down the room. "It was nice while it lasted," he said, "but now it will be even better."

I waited.

"The boss had a swell racket here. A perfect racket. He paid us off well, but I'm going to take over now. The hell with being a cop. It'll make a pretty story, don't you think? I come in here and see you shoot him, then shoot you. Uh-huh, a very pretty story and nobody will blame me. You'll be wrapped up cold for a double murder, first that copper and now him."

"Sure," I said, "but what are you going to do about Grange and her pal?"

Dilwick showed his teeth again. "She's wanted for York's murder, isn't she? Wouldn't it be sweet if they were found dead in a love tryst? The papers would love that. Boy, what a front-page story if *you* don't crowd them off. Grange and her sweetie doing the double Dutch in the drink instead of her cooking for the York kill. That would put a decent end to this mess. I got damn sick and tired of trying to cover up for the boss anyway, and you got in my hair, Hammer."

"Did I?"

"Don't get smart. If I had any sense I would have taken care of you myself instead of letting that dumb bunny of a detective bollix up things when you were tailing me on that back road."

"You wouldn't have done any better either," I spat out.

"No? But I will now." He raised the gun and took deliberate aim at my head.

While he wasted time thumbing back the hammer I tugged the snub-nosed .38 from my waistband that I had taken from the punk with the wrecked face and triggered one into his stomach. His face froze for an instant, the gun sagged, then with all the hatred of his madness he stumbled forward a step, raising his gun to fire.

The .38 roared again. A little blue spot appeared over the bridge of his nose and he went flat on his face.

Mine wasn't the only gun to speak. Outside there was a continual roar of bullets; screams from the house and commands being shouted into the dark. A car must have tried to pull away and smashed into another. More shots and the tinkling of broken glass. A man's voice screamed in agony. A tommy went off in short burps blasting everything in its path. Through the door held open by Mallory's body the brilliant white light of a spotlight turned the night to day and pairs of feet were circling the boathouse.

I shouted, "Price, it's me, Mike. I'm in here!"

A light shot in the door as hands slid the other opening back. A state trooper with a riot gun pointed at me slid in and I dropped the .38. Price came in behind him. "Damn, you still alive?"

"I look it, don't I?" Laughing almost drunkenly I slapped him on the shoulder. "Am I glad to see you! You sure took long enough to get here." Price's foot stretched out and pushed the body on the floor.

"That's . . ."

"Dilwick," I finished. "The other one over there is Mallory."

"I thought you were going to keep me informed on how things stood," he said.

"It happened too fast. Besides, I couldn't be popping in places where I could be recognized."

"Well, I hope your story's good, Mike. It had better be. We're holding people out there with enough influence to swing a state legislature, and if the reason is a phony or even smells like one,

249

you and I are both going to be on the carpet. You for murder."

"Nuts, what was all the shooting about outside?"

"I got your message such as it was and came up here with three cars of troopers. When we got on the grounds a whole squad of mugs with guns in their hands came ripping around the house. They let go at us before we could get out of the cars and there was hell to pay. The boys came up expecting action and they got it."

"Those mugs, chum, were after me. I guess they figured I'd try to make a break for it and circled the house. Dilwick was the only one who knew where we'd be. Hell, he should have. I was after Grange and the Cook girl and he had them in here."

"Now you tell me. Go on and finish it."

I brought him up to date in a hurry. "Dilwick's been running cover for Mallory. When you dig up the books on this joint you're going to see a lot of fancy figures. But our boy Dilwick got ideas. He wanted the place for himself. He shot Mallory with my gun and was going to shoot me, only I got him with the rod I took off the boy whose car I flipped over. Yeah, Dilwick was a good thinker all right. When Grange didn't show up he did what I did and floated down the river himself and found how the eddies took him to the shore. At that time both he and Mallory were figuring on cutting themselves a nice slice of cash from the York estate. Grange was the only one who knew there was evidence that Ruston wasn't

York's son and they were going to squeeze it out of her or turn her over to the police for the murder of York."

Price looked at the body again, then offered me a cigarette. "So Grange really did bump her boss. I'll be a so-and-so."

I lit the butt slowly, then blew the smoke through my nostrils. "Grange didn't bump anybody."

The sergeant's face wrinkled. He stared at me queerly.

"This is the aftermath, Price," I reflected. "It's what happens when you light the fuse."

"What the hell are you talking about?"

I didn't hear him. I was thinking about a kidnapping. I was thinking about a scientist with a cleaver in his skull and the chase on for his assistant. I was thinking about Junior Ghent rifling York's office and coming up with some dirty pictures, and then getting beat up. I was thinking about a shot nicking Roxy and a night with Alice Nichols that might have been fun if it hadn't been planned so my clothes could be searched and my skull cracked afterward. I was thinking about a secret cache in the fireplace, a column in the paper, a cop trying to kill me and some words Mallory told me. I was thinking how all this might have been foreseen by the killer when the killer planned the first kill. I was thinking of the face of the killer.

It was a mess. I had said that a hundred times now, but what a beautiful mess it was. There had never been a mess as nasty as this. Nope, not a dull moment. Every detail seemed to overlap and prod something bigger to happen until you were almost ready to give up, and the original murder was obscured by the craziest details imaginable. Rah, rah, sis boom bah, with a fanfare of trumpets as the police come in and throw bullets all over the place. Was it supposed to end like this? I knew one thing. I was supposed to have died someplace along the line. The killer must be fuming now because I was very much alive. What makes people think they can get away with murder? Some plan it simple, some elaborately extreme, but this killer let things take care of themselves and they wound up better than anyone could have hoped for.

"Don't keep secrets, Mike, who did it?"

I threw the butt down, stamped on it. "I'll tell you tomorrow, Price."

"You'll tell me now, Mike."

"Don't fight me, kid. I appreciate all that you did for me, but I don't throw anyone to the dogs until I'm sure."

"You've killed enough people to be sure. Who was it?"

"It still goes. I have to check one little detail."

"What?"

"Something that makes a noise like a cough."

Price thought I was crazy. "You tell me now or I'll hold you until you do. I can't stick my neck out any further. I'll have hot breaths blowing on my back too, and they'll be a lot hotter if I can't explain this mix-up!"

I was tired. I felt like curling up there with

Dilwick and going to sleep. "Don't squeeze, Price. I'll tell you tomorrow. When you take this little package home . . ." I swept my hand around the room, ". . . you'll get a commendation." Over in the corner a trooper was taking the bonds from the girls. Grange was moaning again. "You can get her side of the story anyway, and that will take care of your superiors until you hear from me."

The sergeant waited a long moment then shrugged his shoulders. "You win. I've waited this long . . . I guess tomorrow will be all right. Let's get out of here."

We carried Grange out together with the other trooper lugging the Cook girl over his shoulder. Myra Grange's pupils were big black circles, dilated to the utmost. She was hopped up to the ears. We got them into one of the police cars then stood around until the casino gang was manacled to each other and the clientele weeded out. I grinned when I spotted a half-dozen Sidon cops in the group. They had stopped bellowing long ago, and from the worried looks being passed around it was going to be a race to see who could talk the loudest and the fastest. There would be a new police force in Sidon this time next week. The public might be simple enough to let themselves be bullied around and their government rot out from underneath them, but it would only go so far. An indignant public is like a mad bull. It wouldn't stop until every tainted employee on the payroll was in a cell. Maybe they'd even give me a medal. Yeah, maybe.

I was sick of watching. I called Price over and told him I was going back. His face changed, but he said nothing. There was a lot he wanted to say, but he could tell how it was with me. Price nodded and let me climb into my car. I backed it up and turned around in the drive. Tomorrow would be a busy day. I'd have to prepare my statements on the whole affair to hand over to a grand jury, then get set to prove it. You don't simply kill people and walk away from it. Hell, no. Righteous kill or not the law had to be satisfied.

Yes, tomorrow would be a busy day. Tonight would be even busier. I had to see a killer about a murder.

Chapter Twelve

It was ten after eleven when I reached the York estate. Henry came out of his gatehouse, saw me and gaped as though he were looking at a ghost. "Good heavens, Mr. Hammer. The police are searching all over for you! You . . . you killed a man."

"So I did," I said sarcastically. "Open the gates."

"No . . . I can't let you come in here. There'll be trouble."

"There will if you don't open the gates." His face seemed to sag and his whole body assumed an air of defeat. Disgust was written in the set of his mouth, disgust at having to look at a man who shot a fellowman. I drove through and stopped.

"Henry, come here."

The gatekeeper shuffled over reluctantly. "Yes, sir?"

"I'm not wanted any longer, Henry. The police have settled the matter up to a certain point."

"You mean you didn't . . ."

"No, I mean I shot him, but it was justified. I've been cleared, understand?"

He smiled a little, not quite understanding, but

he breathed a sigh of relief. At least he knew he wasn't harboring a fugitive in me. I pulled up the driveway to the house, easing around the turns until the beams of my brights spotlighted the house. Inside I saw Harvey coming to the door. Instead of parking in front of the place I rolled around to the side and nosed into the open door of the garage. A big six-car affair, but now there were only two cars in it, counting mine. A long time ago someone started using it for a storeroom and now one end was cluttered with the junk accumulated over the years. Two boys' bicycles were hanging from a suspension gadget set in the ceiling and underneath them a newer model with a small one-cylinder engine built into the frame. Hanging from a hook screwed into an upright were roller skates and ice skates, but neither pair had been used much. Quite a childhood Ruston had.

I shut the door of the garage and looked up. The rain had started. The tears of the gods. Of laughter or sorrow? Maybe the joke was on me, after all.

Harvey was his usual, impeccable, unmoving self as he took my hat and ushered me into the living room. He made no mention of the affair whatsoever, nor did his face reveal any curiosity. Even before he announced me, Roxy was on her way down the stairs with Ruston holding her arm. Billy Parks came out of the foyer grinning broadly, his hand outstretched. "Mike! You sure got your nerve. By gosh, you're supposed to be

Public Enemy Number One!"

"Mike!"

"Hello, Lancelot. Hello, Roxy. Let me give you a hand."

"Oh, I'm no cripple," she laughed. "The stairs get me a little, but I can get around all right."

"What happened, Mike?" Ruston smiled. "The policemen all left this evening after they got a phone call and we haven't seen them since. Golly, I was afraid you'd been shot or something. We thought they caught you."

"Well, they came close, kid, but they never even scratched me. It's all finished. I'm in the clear and I'm about ready to go home."

Billy Parks stopped short in the act of lighting a cigarette. His hands began to tremble slightly and he had trouble finding the tip of the butt.

Ruston said, "You mean the police don't want you any longer, Mike?" I shook my head. He gave a little cry of gladness and ran to me, throwing his arms about me in a tight squeeze. "Gee, Mike, I'm so happy."

I patted his arm and smiled crookedly. "Yep, I'm almost an honest man again."

"Mike . . ."

Roxy's voice was the hoarse sound of a rasp on wood. She was clutching the front of her negligee with one hand, trying to push a streamer of hair from her eyes with the other. A little muscle twitched in her cheek. "Who . . . did it, Mike?"

Billy was waiting, Roxy was waiting. I heard Harvey pause outside the door. Ruston looked from them to me, puzzled. The air in the room was charged, alive. "You'll hear about it tomorrow," I said.

Billy Parks dropped his cigarette.

"Why not now?" Roxy gasped.

I took a cigarette from my pocket and stuffed it between my lips. Billy fumbled for his on the floor and held the lit tip to mine. I dragged the smoke in deeply. Roxy was beginning to go white, biting on her lip. "You'd better go to your room, Roxy. You don't look too good."

"Yes . . . yes. I had better. Excuse me. I really don't feel too well. The stairs . . ." She let it go unfinished. While Ruston helped her up I stood there in silence with Billy. The kid came down again in a minute.

"Do you think she'll be all right, Mike?"

"I think so."

Billy crushed his cig out in an ashtray. "I'm going to bed, Mike. This day has been tough enough."

I nodded. "You going to bed, too, Ruston?"

"What's the matter with everybody, Mike?"

"Nervous, I guess."

"Yes, that's it, I suppose." His face brightened. "Let me play for them. I haven't played since . . . that night. But I want to play, Mike. Will it be all right?"

"Sure, go ahead."

He grinned and ran out of the room. I heard him arrange the seat, then lift the lid of the piano, and the next moment the heavy melody of a classical piece filled the house. I sat down and listened. It was gay one moment, serious the next. He ran up and down the keys in a fantasy of expression. Good music to think by. I chain-lit another cigarette, wondering how the music was affecting the murderer. Did it give him a creepy feeling? Was every note part of his funeral theme? Three cigarettes gone in thought and still I waited. The music had changed now, it was lilting, rolling in song. I put the butt out and stood up. It was time to see the killer.

I put my hand on the knob and turned, stepped in the room and locked the door behind me. The killer was smiling at me, a smile that had no meaning I could fathom. It was a smile of neither defeat nor despair, but nearer to triumph. It was no way for a murderer to smile. The bells in my head were rising in a crescendo with the music.

I said to the murderer, "You can stop playing now, Ruston."

The music didn't halt. It rose in spirit and volume while Ruston York created a symphony from the keyboard, a challenging overture to death, keeping time with my feet as I walked to a chair and sat down. Only when I pulled the .45 from its holster did the music begin to diminish. My eyes never left his face. It died out in a crashing maze of minor chords that resounded from the walls with increased intensity.

"So you found me out, Mr. Hammer."

"Yes."

"I rather expected it these last few days." He

crossed his legs with complete nonchalance and barely a glance at the gun in my hand. I felt my temper being drawn to the brink of unreason, my lips tightening.

"You're a killer, little buddy," I said. "You're a blood-crazy, insane little bastard. It's so damn inconceivable that I can hardly believe it myself, but it's so. You had it well planned, chum. Oh, but you would, you're a genius. I forgot. That's what everyone forgot. You're only fourteen but you can sit in with scientists and presidents and never miss a trick."

"Thank you."

"You have a hair-trigger mind, Ruston. You can conceive and coordinate and anticipate beyond all realm of imagination. All the while I was batting my brain out trying to run down a killer you must have held your sides laughing. You knew pretty well what killing York would expose . . . a series of crimes and petty personalities scrambled together to make the dirtiest omelet ever cooked. But *you'd* never cook for it. Oh, no . . . not you. If . . . if you were found out the worst that could happen would be that you'd face a juvenile court. That's what you thought, didn't you? Like hell.

"Yes, you're only a child, but you have a man's mind. That's why I'm talking to you like I would to a man. That's why I can kill you like I would a man."

He sat there unmoving. If he knew fear he showed it only in the tiny blue vein that throbbed in his forehead. The smile still played around his mouth. "Being a genius, I guess you thought I was stupid," I continued. With every word my heart beat harder and faster until I was filled with hate. "It was getting so that I thought I was stupid myself. Why wouldn't I? Every time I turned around something would happen that was so screwy that it didn't have any place in the plot, yet in a way it was directly related. Junior Ghent and Alice. The Graham boys. Each trying to chop off a slice of cash for themselves. Each one concerned with his own little individual problem and completely unknowing of the rest. It was a beautiful setup for you.

"But please don't think I was stupid, Ruston. The only true stupidity I showed was in calling you Lancelot. If I ever meet the good knight somewhere I'll beg him to forgive me. But I wasn't so stupid otherwise, Ruston. I found out that Grange had something on York . . . and that something was the fact that she was the only one who knew that he was a kidnapper in a sense. York . . . an aging scientist who wanted an heir badly so he could pass on his learning to his son . . . but his son died. So what did he do? He took a kid who had been born of a criminal father and would have been reared in the gutter, and turned him into a genius. But after a while the genius began to think and hate. Why? Hell, only you know that.

"But somewhere you got hold of the details concerning your birth. You knew that York had only a few years to live and you knew, too, that Grange had threatened to expose the entire affair if he didn't leave his money to her. Your father (should I call him that?) was a thinker too. He worked out a proposition with Alice to have an affair with his Lesbian assistant and hold that over her head as a club, and it worked, except that Junior Ghent learned of the affair when his sister told him that York had proposed the same deal to her, too, and Junior wanted to hold that over Grange's head, and Alice's, too, so that he could come in for part of the property split. Man, what a scramble it was after that. Everybody thought I had the dope when it was lying beside the wall out there. Yeah, the wall. Remember the shot you took at Roxy? You were in your room. You tossed that lariat that was beside your bed around the awning hook outside her window, swung down and shot at her through the glass. She had the light on and couldn't see out, but she was a perfect target. You missed at that range only because you were swinging. That really threw me off the track. Nice act you put on when I brought the doctor in. You had him fooled too. I didn't get that until a little while ago.

"Now I know. You, as an intelligent, emotional man were in love. What a howl. In love with your nurse." His face darkened. The vein began to throb harder than ever and his hands clenched into a tight knot. "You shot at her because you saw me and Roxy in a clinch and were jealous. Brother, how happy you must have been when the cops were on my back with orders to shoot to kill. I thought you were simply surprised to see me when I climbed in the window that time. Your face went white, remember? For one second there you thought I came back to get you. That was it, wasn't it?"

His head nodded faintly, but still he said nothing. "Then you saw your chance of bringing the cops charging up by knocking over the lamp. Brilliant mind again. You knew the bulb breaking would sound like a shot. Too bad I got away, wasn't it?

"If I wasn't something of a scientist myself I never would have guessed it. Let me tell you how confounded smart I am. Your time doesn't matter much anyway. I caught up with one of your playmates that snatched you. I beat the living hell out of him and would have done worse to make him talk and he knew it. I'm a scientist at that kind of stuff. He would have talked his head off, only he didn't have anything to say. You know what I asked him? I asked him who Mallory was and he didn't know any Mallory. Good reason too, because ever since you were yanked out of his hands, your father went by the name of Nelson.

"No, he didn't know any Mallory, yet you came home after the kidnapping and said . . . you . . . *heard . . . the . . . name . . . Mallory . . .* mentioned. When I finally got it I knew who the killer was. Then I began to figure how you worked it. Someplace in the house, and I'll find it later, you have the information and Grange's proof that you were Mallory's son. Was it a check that York gave Myra

Grange? Somehow you located Mallory and sent him the clipping out of the back issue in the library and the details on how to kidnap you. That was why the clipping was gone. You set yourself up to be snatched hoping that the shock would kill York. It damn near did. You did it well, too, even to the point of switching Henry's aspirins to sleeping tablets. You set yourself up knowing you could outthink the ordinary mortals on the boat and get away. You came mighty close to failing, pal. I wish you had.

"But when that didn't do it you resorted to murder . . . and what a murder. No sweeter deal could have been cooked up by anyone. You knew that when York heard Mallory's name brought into it he'd think Grange had spilled the works and go hunting up his little pet. You thought correctly. York went out there with a gun, but I doubt if be intended to use it. The rod was supposed to be a bluff. Billy heard York leave, and he heard me leave, but how did you reach the apartment? Let me tell you. Out in the garage there's a motorbike. Properly rigged they can do sixty or seventy any day. The noise like a cough that Billy heard was you, Ruston. The sound of the motorbike, low and throaty. I noticed it had a muffler on it. Yeah, York had a gun, and you had to take along a weapon too. A meat cleaver. When I dreamed up all this I wondered why nobody spotted you going or coming, but it wouldn't be too hard to take to the back roads.

"Ruston, you were born under an evil, lucky

star. Everything that happened after you surprised York in that room and split his skull worked in your favor. Hell seemed to break loose with everybody trying to cut in on York's dough. Even Dilwick. A crooked copper working for Mallory. Your real father needed that protection and Dilwick fitted right in. Dilwick must have guessed at part of the truth without ever really catching on, and he played it to keep Mallory clear and in a good spot to call for a rake-off, but he got too eager. Dilwick's dead and the rest of his lousy outfit are where they're supposed to be, cooling their heels in a cell.

"But where are you? You . . . the killer. You're sitting here listening to me spiel off everything you already know about and you're not a bit worried. Why should you be? Three or four years in an institution for the criminally insane . . . then prove yourself normal and go back into the world to kill again. You have ethics like Grange. There was a woman who probably loved her profession. She loved it so much she saw a chance to further her career by aiding York, then using it as a club to gain scientific recognition for herself.

"But you . . . hell." I spit the word out. "You banked on getting away scot-free first, then as a second-best choice facing a court. Maybe you'd even get a suspended sentence. Sure, why not? Any psychiatrist would see how that could happen. Under the pressure of your studies your mind snapped. Boy, have you got a brain! No chair, not for you. Maybe a couple of years yanked from your lifespan, but what did it matter? You were twenty years ahead of yourself anyway. That was it, wasn't it? Ha!

"Not so, little man. The game just doesn't go that way. I hate to go ex post facto on you, but simply because you're nicely covered by the law doesn't mean you'll stay that way. I'm making up a new one right now. Know what it is?"

He still smiled, no change of expression. It was almost as if he were watching one of his experiments in the rabbit cage.

"Okay," I said, "I'll tell you. All little geniuses . . . or is it genii? . . . who kill and try to get away with it get it in the neck anyway."

Very deliberately I let him see me flick the safety catch on the .45. His eyes were little dark pools that seemed to swim in his head.

I was wondering if I were going to like this.

I never killed a little genius before.

For the first time, Ruston spoke. "About an hour ago I anticipated this," he smiled. I tightened involuntarily. I didn't know why, but I almost knew beforehand what he'd say.

"When I threw my arms around you inside there feigning happiness over your miraculous reappearance, I removed the clip from your gun. It's a wonder you didn't notice the difference in weight."

Did you ever feel like screaming?

My hand was shaking with rage. I felt the hollow space where the clip fitted and swore. I was so damn safety conscious I didn't jack a shell into the chamber earlier either.

And Ruston reached behind the music rack on the piano and came out with the .32.

He smiled again. He knew damn well what I was thinking. Without any trouble I could make the next corpse. He fondled the gun, clicking the hammer back. "Don't move too quickly, Mike. No. I'm not going to shoot you, not just yet. You see, my little knowledge of sleight of hand was quite useful . . . as handy as to know how to open locks. The Normanic sciences weren't all I studied. Anything that presented a problem afforded me the pleasure of solving it in my spare time.

"Move your chair a little this way so I can see you to the best advantage. Ah . . . yes. Compliments are in order, I believe. You were very right and very clever in your deductions. Frankly, I didn't imagine anyone would be able to wade through the tangle that the murder preceded. I thought I did quite well, but I see I failed, up to a certain point. Look at it from my point of view before you invite any impetuous ideas. If you turned me over to the police and proved your case, I would, as you say, stand before a juvenile court. Never would I admit my actual adulthood to them, and I would be sent away for a few years, or perhaps not at all. You see, there's a side to my story too, one you don't know about.

"Or, Mike, and this is an important 'or' . . . I may kill you and claim self-defense. You came in here and in a state of extreme nervous tension hit me. I picked up a gun that dropped out of your pocket . . ." he held up the .32, ". . . and shot you. Simple? Who would disbelieve it, especially with your temperament . . . and my tender years. So sit still and I don't think I'll shoot you for a little while, at least. Before I do anything, I want to correct some erroneous impressions you seem to have.

"I am not a 'few' years ahead of my time . . . the difference is more like thirty. Even that is an understatement. Can you realize what that means? Me. Fourteen years old. Yet I have lived over fifty years! God, what a miserable existence. You saw my little, er, schoolhouse, but what conclusion did you draw? Fool that you were, you saw nothing. You saw no electrical or mechanical contrivances that had been developed by one of the greatest scientific minds of the century. No, you merely saw objects, never realizing what they were for." He paused, grinning with abject hatred. "Have you ever seen them force-feed ducks to enlarge their livers to make better sausages? Picture that happening to a mind. Imagine having the learning processes accelerated through pain. Torture can make the mind do anything when properly presented.

"Oh, I wasn't supposed to actually feel any of all that. It was supposed to happen while I was unconscious, with only the subconscious mind reacting to the incredible pressures being put upon it to grasp and retain the fantastic array of details poured into it like feed being forced through a funnel down a duck's gullet into its belly whether it wants it or not.

"Ah, but who is to say what happens to the mind when such a development takes place? What may happen to the intricate mechanism of the human mind under such stimulation? What new reactions will it develop . . . what new outlets will it seek to repel the monster that is invading it?

"That is how I became what I am . . . but what I learned! I went even farther than was expected of me . . . much farther than the simple sciences and mathematics *he* wanted me to absorb. I even delved into criminology, Mr. Hammer, going over thousands of case histories of past crimes, and when this little . . . circumstance . . . came to my attention, I knew what I had to do . . . then figured out how I could do it.

"I researched, studied and very unobtrusively collected my data, putting myself not *ahead* of you in the commission and solution of criminal actions, but on an approximate level. With your mind highly tuned to absorb, analyze and reconstruct criminal ways, your close association with the police and past experience, you have been able to run a parallel course with me and arrive at the destination at the same time."

He gave me a wry grin. "Or should I say a little behind me?" With his head he indicated the gun in his hand, ". . . seeing that at present I hold the most advantageous position."

I started to rise, but his gun came up. "Remain seated, please. I only said I didn't *think* I would shoot you. Hear me out."

I sat down again.

"Yes, Mr. Hammer, if I had but given it a few days more study your case would have been a hopeless one. Yet you did find me out with all my elaborate precautions, but I still have a marvelous chance to retain my life and liberty. Don't you think?"

I nodded. He certainly would.

"But what good would it do me? Answer me that? What good would it do me? Would I ever have the girl I love . . . or would she have me? She would vomit at the thought. Me, a boy with an adult mind, but still a boy's body. What woman would have me? As the years passed my body would become mature, but the power of my mind would have increased ten-fold. Then I would be an old man within the physical shell of a boy. And what of society? You know what society would do . . . it would treat me as a freak. Perhaps I could get a position as a lightning calculator in a circus. That's what that man did to me! That's what he did with his machines and brilliant thoughts. He crumpled my life into a little ball and threw it in the jaws of science. How I hated him. How I wish I could have made him suffer the way he made me suffer!

"To be twisted on the rack is trivial compared to the way one can be tortured through the mind. Has your brain ever been on fire? Have you ever had your skull probed with bolts of electrical energy while strapped to a chair? Of course not! You can remain smug and commonplace in your normal life and track down criminals and murderers. Your one fear is that of dying. Mine was of not dying soon enough!

"You can't understand how much the human body can suffer punishment. It's like a giant machine that can feed itself and heal its own wounds, but the mind is even greater. That simple piece of sickly gray matter that twists itself into gentle shapes under a thin layer of bone and looks so disarming lying in a bottle of formaldehyde is a colossus beyond conception. It thinks pain! Imagine it . . . it thinks pain and the body screams with the torture of it, yet there is nothing you can call physical in the process. It can conceive of things beyond normal imagination if it is stirred to do so. That is what mine did. Things were forced into it. Learning, he called it, but it might as well have been squeezed into my brain with a compressor, for it felt that way. I knew pain that was not known by any martyr . . . it was a pain that will probably never be known again.

"Your expression changes, Mr. Hammer. I see you believe what I say. You should . . . it is true. You may believe it, but you will never understand it. Right now I can see you change your mind. You condone my actions. I condone them. But would a jury if they knew? Would a judge . . . or the public? No, they couldn't visualize what I have undergone."

Something was happening to Ruston York even as he was speaking. The little-boy look was gone from his face, replaced by some strange metamorphosis that gave him the facial demeanor I had seen during the wild mouthings of dictators. Every muscle was tense, veins and tendons danced under the delicate texture of his skin and his eyes shone with the inward fury that was gnawing at his heart.

He paused momentarily, staring at me, yet somehow I knew he wasn't really seeing me at all. "You were right, Mr. Hammer," he said, a new, distant note in his voice now. "I *was* in love with my nurse. Or better . . . I am in love with . . . Miss Malcom. From the moment she arrived here I have been in love with her."

The hard, tight expression seemed to diminish at the thought and a smile tugged faintly at the corners of his mouth. "Yes, Mr. Hammer, love. Not the love a child would give a woman, but a man's love. The kind of love you can give a woman . . . or any other normal man."

Suddenly the half-smile vanished and the vacant look came back again. "That's what that man did to me. He made an error in his calculations, or never expected his experiment to reach such a conclusion, but that man did more than make me a mental giant. He not only increased my intellectual capacity to the point of genius . . . but in the process he developed my emotional status until I was no longer a boy.

"I am a man, Mr. Hammer. In every respect except this outer shell, and my chronological age, I am a man. And I am a man in love, trapped inside the body of a child. Can you imagine it? Can you think of me presenting my love to a woman like Roxy Malcom? Oh, she might understand, but never could she return that love. All I would get would be pity. Think of that . . . pity. That's what that bastard did to me!"

He was spitting the words out now, his face back in the contours of frustration and hatred, his eyes blankly looking at me, yet through me. It had to be like this, I thought, when he was on the brink of the deep end. It was the only chance I had. Slowly, I tucked my feet under me, the movement subtle so as not to distract him. I'd probably take a slug or two, but I'd lived through them before and if I managed it right I might be able to get my hands on his gun before he could squeeze off a fatal one. It was the only chance I had. My fingers were tight on the arms of the chair, the muscles in my shoulders bunched to throw myself forward . . . and all the time my guts were churning because I knew what I could expect before I could get all the way across that room to where he was sitting.

"I have to live in a world of my own, Mr. Hammer. No other world would accept me. As great a thing, a twisted thing that I am, I have no world to live in."

The blankness suddenly left his eyes. He was seeing me now, seeing what I was doing and knowing what I was thinking. His thumb pulled back the hammer on the .32 to make it that much easier to trigger off. Behind the now almost colorless pupils of his eyes some crazy thought was etching itself into his mind.

Ruston York looked at me, suddenly with his boy-face again. He even smiled a tired little smile and the gun moved in his hand. "Yes," he repeated, "as great as I am, I am useless."

Even while he had talked, he had done something he had never done before. He exposed himself to himself and for the first time saw the futility that was Ruston York. Once again he smiled, the gun still on me.

There was no time left at all. It had to be now, *now!* Only a second, perhaps, to do it in.

He saw me and smiled, knowing I was going to do it. "Sir Lancelot," he said wistfully.

Then, before I could even get out of the chair, Ruston York turned the gun around in his hand, jammed the muzzle of it into his mouth and pulled the trigger.